THE BOY IN THE MONKEY

a novella by

ANIL KURUKULASOORIYA

CW01500492

•

NAT 1 PUBLISHING

a literary nonprofit corporation

Books that make you question your choices.

THE BOY IN THE MONKEY
Copyright © 2025 by Anil Kurukulasooriya
Produced by Nat 1 Publishing, a literary nonprofit
www.nat1publishing.com
All rights reserved
v.1: 03.22.2025

ISBN: 9798306784892

Cover Art and Design by B.S.Roberts
Edits by Kathleen Locke and B.S.Roberts
Title./Header Font: "Atomosfer" by Heroglyphs Studio
Interior Font: "EB Garamond 12" by Georg Duffner

Opinions expressed in this publication are those of the author. They do not purport to reflect the opinions or views of the publishing house or its members. The publisher does not have any control over and does not assume any responsibility for author or third-party websites, social media, or their content.

This book is dedicated to my family.

I began writing it as a remembrance of absent loved ones but finished it as a gift for my children.

i
MY NAME iS...

I awoke with warmth on my brow and was immediately conscious of someone stroking my head. *Is it Ashley?* Yes—most likely, it was the love of my life. The touch of her hand reminds me of when my mother used to rub my head as a child. The reassuring rub of a woman's hand on your head is about as comforting as a touch between humans can be.

A drop of cold liquid hit me between the eyes. My slumber and drowsiness abruptly ended, and my senses reawoke. My eyes focus on the offending leaf above my head. *Is that leaf-print wallpaper?* No, they are real leaves. *Why is there foliage in my bedroom?* I realized that different shades and shapes of green surround my immediate environment. It appears someone is carrying me through some kind of forest or wood. *What is going on?* I must have fainted, but is someone cradling me?

I remembered the astonishing truth as reality flooded back into my mind—the person cradling me was my mother, but it was not my birth mother! Although a stroke to the head is a comfort regularly used by people, it is also used by animals. Please make every effort to understand this confusing tale; my body is very weak, and I am extremely young. After the accident, and since I found myself in these new circumstances, my mind finds it difficult to make sense of this reality. The caress on my head feels so warm and protective. I could sleep for another week with that furry hand on my head.

But I had to concentrate to figure out what this place was and why I was there. I was a twenty-year-old student living in London, loving a Turkish woman and part of a family. I still have the mind of that twenty-year-old student, but this ain't Kansas, or at least East London, where my family lives. Some people say

London is a jungle, but they should try actually living in the *real* jungle for two weeks!

This had been the longest fourteen days of my lives. The heat was so intense during the day that I tended to nap in my nest. The humidity means the air is thick and can rain for what seems like days. There was a cacophony of noise during the evening, like an orchestra of deaf musicians playing with their instruments. When darkness descends in this foreign environment, the unknown is terrifyingly intimidating. I stared out into obscurity, trying to figure out where the place was, but my second mother could sense my fear. When I trembled, she held me tight and made reassuring grunts to settle my whimpers. The stroke of her furry hand on my forehead calms me and is a potent sleep inducer.

Whatever this place is—reality or fiction—it was a confusing cycle of chaos. *Where is my girlfriend? Why am I separated from my family in these bizarre circumstances? How could it be that weeks ago, I was a person who bought groceries from the supermarket, but this morning, drank warm milk from a hairy teat.*

Certain thoughts kept repeatedly looping in my nightmares. There was a violent accident. I could not remember if I was in a plane or a car, but I remember a collision and being taken underwater. I was unable to breathe and suffocated. As the water filled my lungs, I remembered fear, immense sadness, and my last thoughts were of resignation.

My body and mind felt like a herd of rampaging elephants had hit them. I was the cricket ball, and Vivian Richards had just hit me for six out of the stadium! *Ladies and gentlemen, we have just witnessed a monstrous hit!* The profound impact of this event was so powerful it separated my soul from my body. My disorientated consciousness drifted into nothingness for an unknown period. Seconds, hours, weeks, and years could have passed, and the only thing my sanity could cling to was the murmurings of life from another reality. Certain otherworldly noises echoed around me. The sounds of someone weeping and muffled cries. I felt a pressing sensation on my hand that was no longer present, in the same way an amputee experiences phantom limb pain. Apart from these fragments of existence, I felt like a solitary grain of sand. Alone in an empty universe with no substance and devoid of life.

That is when my savior appeared for the first time. He was an unexpected potential rescuer from obscurity. My little monkey brother was smiling on the shore. It felt like I had to swim through the treacle of a murky lake. He was calling me, not with human words but instead with primate calls and playful gibber, clamoring for me to join him as his playmate. He knew I desperately needed help, and anything was better than this black lake, so I swam toward him. His aura was a golden beacon in bleak obscurity, a baby monkey willing me through the darkness.

I swam through the desolate lake, churning through the fourth dimension, taking a breath of imaginary air after every two strokes. He drew me to shore, and his name became palpable as we neared. *Branko*, my little monkey sibling.

As I approached him, he cartwheeled with glee. He knew he was being reunited with his eternal playmate, and he danced and rolled with delight. He grabbed my hand when I touched shore and pulled me onto land. We rolled on the floor like two polar bear cubs cuddling for warmth. Back together with the yin monkey and my yang human, we would never part again.

From that moment, we were one.

My second mother's name was Aliba, and she cared for me for every second of the last two weeks. The name from my previous life is irrelevant. Here, our name is Branko.

We need to grow and get stronger. Part of my former identity remains, scraps and shreds of the person from London who needs to know what happened in his previous life. I am a twenty-year-old boy sharing a monkey's soul and body. That is not how I pictured spending the year 2000.

Two central purposes remain: to return to my true love and a promise to look after my family. Only God knows what they will do when a monkey walks into their living room and tries to hug them!

I must get back to them, but not just yet. The sweet bananas in this forest are heavenly, and I am living in the body of a baby monkey. We have a long trip ahead, and strength will be essential to make it.

2
FOREST LIVING

Being Branko was not natural, yet it felt more like me every time we woke. With every passing minute, I felt as if the essence of the human was evaporating. It was like being born again when I first awakened in this little primate's body. I cannot remember life in my original mother's tummy, but I can remember the Nothing that existed before waking as Branko.

The feeling of being a boy in a monkey's body seemed to diminish with every new experience. I have lived as a monkey for two months now. The mornings commence with stretching and looking out on the forest as the sun rises. My mother taught me to swing on a vine, locate delicious insects, and pee off the canopy onto the forest floor. These were unusual experiences for a student from London, but they were fascinating, and part of me wanted to forget previous memories like reading boring books at the university library.

Branko's spirit carried me through any anxiety or hesitation. We lived this journey as a partnership and utilized our individual skills for the relevant task. When a bug needed to be eaten or a bottom required cleaning with a stick, Branko would take the reins. However, if I am absolutely truthful, when we peed on a jaguar cub's head last week, that was pretty much my idea. However, when we took a dump in a hippo's mouth, *that* was all Branko.

My human mind was checkered like a chessboard. There were so many holes in my memory it was difficult to piece any meaningful remembrances together. The boy in the monkey retained one sole objective that drove me on through the jungle to an unknown conclusion: to prove to my family and my girlfriend that I was still alive and that love could conquer the obstructions separating us. Therefore, it was essential to devise a plan to leave this place.

Six months had passed since Aliba had given birth to Branko. I figured this out as Aliba used a stone to mark our home tree bark with a cross every six days. It was not clear why six days is significant on the monkey calendar. Five marks made a month, and she has made thirty marks since my arrival.

Each morning, Aliba woke to forage, but not before covering me with leaves that made a camouflaged blanket. She returned with a breakfast fit for a king, including wholesome leaves, fruit, seeds, tree bark, plant bulbs, and flowers. The plant bulbs were so juicy and cleansed the palate before a tangy, crunchy termite. One favorite mother-and-son pastime was sucking up termite-shakes. There was a very specific approach to lure out the insects for a delectable feast. First, we found a suitable stick and inserted it into the termite nest. Then we poked around until the termites got really annoyed. They would start running up the stick or out of their nest, and then you gobbled them up. On certain occasions, I have eaten fifty in one sitting, but this can lead to serious indigestion and, on one occasion, termite diarrhea!

After meals, primate dental hygiene required brushing teeth with a twig and ensuring a regular constitution by curling out a good poop. Mum even insisted on flossing using some hair from my fur, but removing the hair was almost as unpleasant as flossing using it. Sometimes the thought went through my head, *I am not an animal,* but then I cleaned my arse with the same twig I brushed my teeth, and I realized times have changed.

Aliba taught me how to maneuver around the jungle. She showed me essential skills like which branch was safe to swing on, which berries were safe to eat, and which rocks hid a veritable feast of insect life beneath them. She was a survival expert, and with her by my side, I had nearly no worries.

However, there was always some lingering threat in the jungle. Our most pressing concern was being stalked by a trio of ominous monkeys. They seemed to be following our movements around the jungle, and we hadn't been able to shake them for the past four days. It was unclear if this was typical behavior, but Aliba seemed agitated. They were inquisitive fellows with distinctive characteristics; one had a particularly large bottom, another only one arm, and the third had what can only be described as a handlebar mustache (it curled up at the corners, and I was convinced he must use ear wax to style it). I called them the *three Hs:* Huge Bottom, Harmless, and Handlebar.

They have kept a safe distance from us, but their presence is increasingly threatening. From my limited knowledge of male monkeys stalking females, this doesn't bode well. Aliba being stalked means they have her scent. This meant they thought she might be ready to mate. Mating monkeys don't tend to have much time for baby monkeys as they tend to ruin the amorous gang-rape mood. If they came at us, it was likely their attack would end in my death and the brutal violation of my mother. This may be normal in the animal kingdom, but it was not normal for me.

Last night, they threw a few stones in our direction to test the water. After four days of surveillance, they had likely determined that no male was returning to protect us, so this gang was getting far more boisterous. Initially, I thought they were cheeky monkeys, but their presence had become menacing, and an attack seemed imminent. Aliba was a warrior queen, but she couldn't withstand an attack from three males. I am small, weak, and more of a hindrance than assistance to Aliba. My focus has been on how to get back to England, but there was a more pressing worry to focus on. We needed a plan on how to help survive another day.

Something I have seen on our travels around the forest had given me hope. We traveled west of our home tree yesterday, and I had a vision from my past that meant humans shared this forest. Salvation was round, yellow, numerous, and moving along the forest floor. It looked like dozens of yellow beetles crawling along the ground. However, upon dropping down through the canopy of the jungle, I was surrounded by foreign mechanical noises. Saws slaughtered the trees, and when they ceased their murder, men shouted a familiar phrase in my former language, "*Timber!*"

Round yellow beetles meant hard hats for logging. Whilst I was mesmerized by seeing my former fellow man, the monkey in me was disgusted by the ruin of the forest. Aliba descended to my vantage point and gave me a crack round the head for approaching the humans. The fear in her eyes was obvious, and I did not want to upset her any longer, so I followed her back up through the trees using my much-improved vine-swinging technique.

Tomorrow, when Aliba goes foraging, I will leave the confines of our home tree and my leaf blanket and head toward the humans. I am not sure what I will find, but Aliba and I need something to protect us from the three Hs. Handlebar looks like a particularly demented monkey, and I want to be prepared when he comes knocking on our door or tree. Without some sort of protection, we were sitting duck-monkeys.

3
MONKEY OR BOY?

I was consumed with worry about the past, present, and future. Every day was tough in this environment, but I knew tomorrow could be our last chance for salvation. The stress was relentless, knowing that any day could be our last. *How do I fashion a means of protection with such primitive materials?* The worries consuming my thoughts throughout the day had exhausted my young body. The gentle rocking of my mother lulled me into a false sense of security, and I drifted into slumber. After all, I was just a boy residing in the body of a young monkey.

I looked to my left, and Ashley lay beside me! In a way that she finds slightly creepy, I have watched her sleep so many times. I used to relish arising in the morning and watching her sleep or, by chance, waking suddenly in the night and seeing the moonlight upon her face. As I watched, the first rays of the morning sun illuminated her. There are tiny speckles of eyeliner in her eyelashes that she has failed to clean away before getting into bed. I stroke her face, and she smiles and rubs against me like a contented cat. Something tickles her nose as she rubs up against my body, and she sneezes.

She woke abruptly, and even her half-open eyes could not hide her horror. She hurls herself backward away from me, screaming and lashing out with kicks and swipes of her arms. I tried to control her wild swinging limbs, but she started screaming hysterically. I tried to speak, but only panic-fueled cries escaped my mouth. I started jumping on the bed. I bared my teeth—a common gesture when my kind are agitated.

Then, I noticed my claws had drawn blood when I attempted to calm her as she flung her arms at me. I stepped back from her, shocked at the sudden change in mood, staggered that I had been capable of injuring her. Weren't we happily lying together just moments ago?

Desperate for an escape, I turned and faced the mirror in our bedroom to see what had garnered this reaction from my lover. The elongated arms, black furry body, clear pale skin on my face, large nostrils and ears, and furrowed jutting brow. Monkeys and humans share ninety-nine percent of the same DNA, they resemble humans so closely but not so much that you want to wake up in bed with one.

I turned back to face her, but the room disintegrated. The four walls of my bedroom become a mirrored box reflecting my image in every direction. Confronted with my human body and no fur to hide behind, for the first time in my life, I felt truly naked. For the past six months, I had walked the forest without a stitch or even an Adam-like leaf. Yet, in this mirror box, there was no way of concealing my absurd human form. Branko's body felt safe and protected, and I yearned for a return to my monkey shell. The former human carcass that I inhabited for twenty years felt vulnerable and weak. It was no longer durable enough for the challenges ahead. It was too soon to return to my old shoes. Perhaps those shoes would never fit again?

I blinked, and the surroundings of the mirrored box disappeared, leaving me in Aliba's safe grip again. The dream left me even more restless, but I needed to sleep as the next day would decide our future. Fate did not care if it was monkey or boy resided in this body, as both could die just as easily.

4
MONKEY ROBBERY

S leep has been difficult to come by, and I had been up since sunrise. The morning had been full of apprehension and pessimism, which had carried over from the night before. I considered leaving the nest before Aliba woke but couldn't bear to put her through so much worry wondering where I had disappeared to. Our eyes had been on the surrounding trees for most of the morning, and we had yet to see the three Hs. Their absence reassured me a little such that I was slightly less reluctant to leave Aliba. When she leaves the nest, I will head west. She kissed my forehead softly, covered me with some leaves, and bounded off the tree, flying to catch a vine. She was away, and shortly after her exit, I was too.

To the north, there was an enormous mountain visible in the distance. I have considered the route in my mind throughout the night and have trodden the path repeatedly in my sleep. Now, I was traversing it for real, and I felt sluggish. Last night, this journey in my head was effortless, but the reality was exhausting.

Aliba had not allowed Branko to travel independently due to the numerous dangers in the jungle. For that reason, this journey was exciting but also treacherous. There were certain flag posts that guided me to the desired destination. Left at the massive tree and straight past the sloth who never seemed to move, along the vines in the canopy for a few hundred meters, then down and onto an old rickety bridge. The journey was only about fifteen minutes in total, but due to the tension, it felt overwhelming and arduous.

As I approached the flimsy crossing, I realized this overpass was like something out of an *Indiana Jones* movie. Why did my checkered memory remember useless eighties movie facts yet be unable to recall my name? The bridge crossed the river about fifty meters above the level of the white water. Both monkey and boy were nervous about crossing this platform due to our cumulative lack of swimming ability, but time was of the essence. The clearing containing the humans was only a short swing past the bridge. Fear needed to be overcome to make this journey as efficient as possible.

As I stepped onto the bridge and looked down, I saw it was pockmarked with holes. Take my advice: *never crouch down and peer through the holes.* Rapidly moving white water and rapids swept beneath my feet. It was a close call regarding whether the human or the monkey would be a better swimmer. A fall from this height into that water meant another watery death. Given that my last life ended by drowning, I was keen to avoid a repeat. At moments of intense pressure, it was inevitable that paranoia would kick in. *Is that a crocodile down there in the water?*

The last time I saw a crocodile was at London Zoo when I visited with my brother Amal and his daughter Ava. This sudden realization popped into my head. I have a brother called Amal and a niece called Ava! *I have a brother called Amal and a niece called Ava!* I said it over and over in my head. I started doing a little celebration dance, forgetting my present circumstances. A sidestep, a twist, a moonwalk too far! My right leg hovered over the gap as I regained my mental and physical composure. *Remember the task at hand. To get back to your family, you must cross this bridge and meet the humans.*

I looked down through the gap again and saw that the green I mistook for a crocodile was, in fact, a piece of plastic. Probably litter from the human settlement ahead. I hopped over the bridge, realizing how much more limber I was as a monkey than a human. I was always quite heavy-footed as a homosapien. I crossed the bridge and climbed up the nearest tree. It was much safer in the trees than down amongst the ground folk. A few swings, and I could hear the mechanical mayhem of the deforesters. Branko's anxiety grew at being surrounded by the unnatural noise, but my composure was enough to settle his nerves. From scanning the horizon, I saw and tracked the first yellow hat. He was twenty feet below me, but even from this distance, I could still tell he was extremely fat. He was spraying trees with red paint, marking those to be executed or spared capital punishment. Just another day on death row for these trees. It was ironic that they didn't commit a crime but were condemned to death, and yet they endured their sentence with such dignity.

Suddenly, what I was looking for appeared magically before me. The fat yellow hat had finished marking his territory and had walked down a trail to what appeared to be the largest cabin in the complex. To my right, trees were being felled by the dozen. Teams of men cut, lifted, and moved logs onto lorries to be transported out of the forest. The tree harvest was the saddest sight imaginable. It was the equivalent of tree genocide. Would I have felt this way before I was a monkey? I didn't even use recycled paper as a human—now I used the same twig for my teeth and my bottom. Branko and I were becoming one with the repercussion that I was more aligned with nature and my environment.

I crept through the trees and settled by the cabin. It was extremely large and looked like a trailer from a lorry converted into a workspace, but it only had one door. However, there were many windows, and one had to be open in this heat. With the stealth of a thief, I climbed down the tree, hopped onto the guttering of the cabin, and edged around the perimeter until I found an open window. Being a monkey burglar was much more efficient than the cat variety. I looked in through the window and saw a fat yellow-hatted man being berated by another man in a shirt and tie. The room must have been hot because sweat dripped off the angry man's forehead. He sure was ugly when he shouted in fury. In fact, he would be ugly no matter what his emotional state. The irritated, ugly man was almost completely bald and held a cigarette in his right hand. His armpits were sweaty, and sweat flew off his arms as he gesticulated. A droplet landed on the fat man's face as he was being castigated. The meaty man reminded me of a sad bear being scolded because he didn't want to dance in the circus. Perhaps this forest was the circus, and its destruction was the meaningless dance?

The ugly—and now furious—man threw down his cigarette and stamped on it. The portly man jumped up from his seat, and they both marched out of the office. Pudgy was followed by his senior. This was my chance, and I seized the opportunity to enter the room and steal something of value. The potential weapon was positioned on the ugly man's desk: a knife of some kind. As the item came nearer, I recognized it was a letter opener. Having entered the office through a louver, I descend the curtain and hop onto the table. I slip on a piece of paper, and a thought occurred to me as I reached for the knife. *I can leave a message on the paper for one of the humans.*

As I lifted the pen, I considered what to write. Perhaps, *Help! I was a boy, but now my soul is trapped in a monkey's body* ? That might be a little too much for the recipient to process. Something simpler like, *Please help me*, will have to suffice. I get as far as the word *Help* when a glimmer of light shone in my eye. I followed the light to its source and saw a golden square object. Now, *that* item was much more useful than a letter opener. I picked it up, flicked the wheel of the zippo, and monkey had created fire! This primate had just jumped about one million years in the evolutionary chain!

At that moment, the door flew open. It was time for quick thinking. The ugly bald man strode in, and it was fair to say he was surprised to see a monkey sitting on his desk with a lighter aflame. We paused and stared at each other like gunfighters before a showdown.

He made his sudden and aggressive intentions clear by reaching down to his left and raising an umbrella vigorously. There was no time for negotiation, so I flicked the lighter cap and switched off the flame. I glimpsed down to my right and saw a bowl of pushpins. Grabbing a handful, I started flinging the pins at his hideous face.

A blow struck his nose, and he staggered backward. He swiped the umbrella at me, but my superpower monkey agility meant I avoided the blow. As I hopped away, another attempted smash narrowly missed my leg. That blow was too close for comfort.

I fired a handful of remaining tacks at his face. He opened the umbrella, and his vision was obscured. Whilst he was blinded, I climbed the curtain and escaped out of the louver. He bellowed and walloped the window with the brolly.

This time, he didn't get close to my swiftly disappearing bottom. By the time he was out of the hut, I had escalated up a tree trunk and scarpered to a safe distance. At a certain height, I was totally obscured by his vantage point on the ground. Due to the stress levels of the experience, I gave myself a few seconds to calm down as my heart raced, but the risk was worth taking. In my left hand was a golden lighter. This was the type of weapon that could ensure my new family's safety.

I needed to get back to my nest as I had been away for at least thirty minutes, and Aliba would be back at any moment. When she sifted through my bedding to find only leaves, she would be terrified. *I need to get back*. The three Hs won't be far away, and Aliba desperately needed me.

5
MUMBO JUMBO

It was surprising how, when I reached the rickety rope bridge for the return journey, I crossed without hesitation. Adrenalin coursed through my veins after the confrontation in the cabin that quickened my journey back to Aliba. She may have returned to the nest, but so might the three Hs. The thought of her alone with Huge Bottom, Harmless, and Handlebar sent a shiver through me. However, the zippo lighter in my hand boosted my belief in being able to protect my mother.

When stepping off the bridge, I was confronted by an unusual sight. Obstructing my return to Aliba was an elephant with one of his front legs raised, and he appeared to be requesting me to stop. From the size of this beast, I could tell he was an immature animal. Not a child anymore but also not yet an adult. He was somewhere in between, and although I realized this teenage mammal required my assistance, I urgently wanted to get back to my vulnerable parent. Unfortunately, the creature was blocking my escape up to the trees. When I tried to run around this brute, he pushed me back onto the bridge. It appeared my progress was not permitted until I provided him with help.

Strangely, the confrontation with this elephant reminded me of my past. Why is that name familiar? I had a friend called Nelly back in London! He was one of my best school friends, and I had known him since I was a young boy. He was half Indian and half English. His Indian grandmother gave him the most ridiculous name I have ever heard—Nishpunk. We called him Nelly instead because otherwise, people laughed at his real name. I decided this elephant in front of me should be called Nishpunk, too.

Using monkey chatter, I addressed Nishpunk and requested he move aside. The monkey puffed up his body whilst growling and hissing at this great beast. I bared my teeth and scraped dirt on the ground in front of me. Nishpunk didn't seem too intimidated, and in response, he tapped his still-raised front leg with his trunk and then made the most terrifying rumble. My body trembled as both Branko, and I quickly realized that brains and not brawn were required to find a solution. This crazed elephant was preventing our return to Aliba.

I decided to step toward Nishpunk slowly, as he might allow me to pass. As I did, he started waving his foreleg. Upon a closer inspection of the raised leg, I realized Nishpunk wasn't waving his foot at me to signal *stop*, he was trying to show me something lodged between his toes.

It seemed this erratic elephant was a clumsy and accident-prone fellow. He had stepped on a sharp stone that was stuck between the toes of his foot. This looked extremely painful, and it seemed he required help to remove the object. I vaguely remembered a biology lesson in secondary school relating to crocodiles forming symbiotic relationships with birds. The birds would sit in the crocodile's mouth and clean away fragments of meat, somewhat like an ornithological dentist! I couldn't immediately recall reading about monkeys acting as podiatrists, though!

Nishpunk stepped back nervously when I approached his foot. I gestured for him to come to me and gently stroked his trunk. He settled down and lowered his foot. The sharp-edged stone was lodged quite deeply into the bottom of his huge foot. Some sort of stick was needed to leverage the stone out. I found an appropriately sized fallen branch from the forest edge and gently placed it between the stone and Nishpunk's foot.

When I looked him in the eye, I saw a poor, frightened animal. I gestured with my fingers on *one, two, three,* and simultaneously displayed the numbers with my fingers. I waved my finger, *one,* and Nishpunk closed one eye. I gestured two and quickly flicked the stick. The stone came out with little fuss, and Nishpunk was still waiting for me to count to three! He opened his eyes, and I pointed to the stone on the floor. Nishpunk trumpeted with a joyful blast.

Unfortunately, there wasn't time to celebrate with my new friend. I hopped onto the elephant's back and then jumped onto a vine. Ten minutes of swinging, and I would be past the sloth and almost home. However, when I reached the sloth's home, I discovered that he had absconded (technically, it is impossible for a sloth to abscond because they are so slow). What could have persuaded him to move from his favorite area of rest? As I considered the permutations, I heard the answer. A blood-curdling primate scream echoed around me. It was combined with the violent cries of the other attacking monkeys, and I was certain Aliba was in immense peril. The only comfort I could glean was that her cries meant she was alive, but what were those animals doing to her?

As I approached the nest, I could see she was surrounded. My monkey mother had a wild look in her eyes. She was a formidable protector and looked ready to confront all three Hs. Her insane fury seemed to be multiplied by my disappearance. Harmless barked at her, and she smashed him in the face with a clenched fist. She hissed at Huge Bottom and then jumped on him, sinking her nails into his arms. Handlebar, seeing an opportunity, leaped onto her exposed back. She yelped with pain as he ripped at her arm. I needed to help her and end this battle swiftly before Aliba was even more seriously hurt.

As I jumped onto the branch leading to my family nest, I let out the loudest bark I could muster. The three Hs immediately stopped their assault on my mother. She lay wounded on the ground, but I detected movement in her chest. She was breathing and raised her head to look at me. A brief reassuring smile was followed by a harrowing look of pain. The worry for her baby was obvious, and the tension in the jungle air seemed as thick as a rhino's hide. Time slowed, and each second seemed pivotal. I stood up as tall as my legs would allow and adopted the most aggressive stare, knowing that any sign of weakness in my body could make my vulnerable position even more precarious.

The three Hs formed a triangle in front of me and began cackling with glee. Like three hairy witches about to boil a child in a cauldron, they anticipated a minor's impending doom. I let them get close and then wielded my nuclear weapon. It then occurred to me that these monkeys may not be afraid of fire.

As I flicked the lighter and showed them my magical power, all three Hs stopped in their tracks as the monkey magician bamboozled them! Seeing their hesitation, I doubled down and started chanting mumbo jumbo to increase their confusion.

Wielding my lightsaber confidently, I jabbed forward with my weapon, causing Harmless and Huge Bottom to fall backward. Handlebar stood his ground, so I threatened him again, but he wasn't in the slightest bit afraid of the flame or my monkey jibber jabber.

Handlebar made the mistake of leaning toward me, hypnotized by the light of the flame. Even though the proximity of this psychopathic primate was butt-clenchingly intimidating, I knew immediately that it was my chance.

Mesmerized by the flickering flame, Handlebar came a little too close, and as his curled mustache touched the heat, it ignited like tinder. The left curl of his mustache evaporated, and his face suddenly looked strangely imbalanced, half of his whiskers were reduced to dust.

He cartwheeled backward in shock and yelped with pain. As he stared incredulously at my powerful weapon, I couldn't help but laugh at his lopsided look. I waved the flame at the three of them again, and they fled. Huge Bottom and Harmless ran away arm in arm as Handlebar fell off the tree trunk and through the canopy. As he moved through the trees, he swung on a vine with one arm and covered his mouth with the other.

I doubted we would be seeing the three Hs for a while. The only remnants of them was the smell of burnt monkey hair.

I looked at my monkey mother who was now standing. She limped whilst smiling and gave me a warm embrace as she kissed the top of my head. Within her embrace, I began checking her body for injuries. Her arm was grazed but none of her abrasions were serious. She smothered me, rubbing my body and kissing my face, overcome by the elation due to survival after such a close brush with death. Then her expression changed, with her brow furrowed and lips puckered. First, she pointed at the golden lighter and barked with anger and confusion. Not wanting to upset her further, I hopped past her and placed the lighter in our nest.

She pointed at the nest and made a circle with her hands. The nest was empty on her return from foraging. I lowered my head in shame as I wasn't sure how to explain where I had been. Aliba picked me up and gave me a pretend smack on the bottom. We giggled and pretended to wrestle whilst sharing a desperate hug. She was the most loving mother a boy could ever hope for.

As we embraced, I remembered I was not a boy, and this wasn't my first mother. This realization tempered my happiness. This was a temporary home, and I have a duty to Aliba, but I also had my family back in England. My memory of them was not diminishing, if anything it was becoming clearer. I knew I had to return to find out what happened to me. At present I was content in the body of a baby monkey with a primate mother caring for me. However, if my full memory returned, would I be able to continue living in this confinement? This was not a time for deep thought, as I wanted to celebrate the day's success. I planned and executed a complex monkey burglary, performed an operation on a sick elephant, and managed to stage a demonstration of fire magic to an audience of four primates. Today, I saved my mother's life and my own. We would feast to mark the vanquishing of an enemy. I deserved a termite shake and a belly full of berries as a reward for winning this battle, but the war continued.

6
MIRROR VIEW

It was sunrise, and Aliba had already departed the nest searching for food. I stared into the distance and saw the sun creeping over the horizon. Morning in the jungle was a luxury for my senses. The smell of overnight rain mixed with the vibrant colors of the jungle landscape.

Something unusual stood out in the distance. I could see a light flashing in a tree. It almost looked like a dot, dot, dash, dash, and dot. *Is that a pattern?* I was never a good Cub Scout, but it looked like Morse code. *I need to get to that light!*

I swung through the jungle vines and realized the light was flickering and losing vitality. It was getting weaker as I approached it. I missed a vine and grasped at the air, desperately searching for a replacement creeper. My heart leaped into my throat, but the panic subsided as I steadied my progress by grasping at a piece of vegetation that supported my weight. I focused on the diminished glimmer and was magnetically drawn to its gentle glint.

The light was much higher in the canopy than in my position—I could see a twinkle directly above me but needed to climb to reach it. As I reached the level of the light, I peered through the leaves to find that the flashing originated from a small circular mirror. I pick up the mirror and stared inside the looking glass, wondering what Branko would find there. Unexpectedly, instead of a monkey face, a surprised human face was reflected back.

Blinking repeatedly in shock at my reflection, I closed my eyes, hoping that when I reopened them, I would perceive a more palatable reality. However, when I did open them, I was no longer in a tree but in a totally different world.

•••

I am standing at the front door of a very familiar abode. This is unmistakeably the door to my family house! The opening is ajar and without a moment's hesitation, I step through in search of my family. I am home! *I am home!*

The narrow corridor entrance to my house leads straight for about seven feet before a right turn brings you to our family kitchen. The scent of my mum's curried lamb fills my nostrils as I approach the room that is her domain. I've smelt so many delicious meals emanating from this kitchen over the years, and the familiar scent of one of my favorite dishes proves the authenticity of this place. I see a glimpse of a black cat running up the stairs, and I chase after Sooty boy!

I run up the stairs and am on the second floor's landing. No sign of my little feline friend. I look straight ahead and see the drying cupboard. The door is slightly open, which makes me think Sooty is hiding in there.

In my youth, I used to frequently find him snoozing in the warmth of this cupboard. I open the door and am stunned by the sight of a snarling tiger. Its orange stripes glow in the darkness of the space. The tiger seems impossibly big for the confined area. Due to the squeeze of its surroundings, it cannot quickly pounce on the foolish person who has clumsily stumbled into range.

Saliva drips from his exposed fangs, and he is readying himself to pounce. He is coiled to attack and readies his hips to strike. I take a seemingly last gasp of air and stare into the cold, soulless eyes of the beast. He leaps.

The door of the cupboard swings shut and the danger is extinguished. I hear the impact of the tiger on the door, and then a roar of frustration emanates from the cupboard, shaking the house's foundations.

My mum walks through the living room door onto the landing and addresses me, "Can you please remember to close the drying cupboard? Otherwise, Sooty sleeps on the towels and leaves fur all over them! Where have you been? Lunch is ready for you and your dad wants to have a chat with you upstairs. I think he is worried about how much you have been away recently. He thinks you are forgetting about us."

I stare at her, astounded and stricken mute by the shock of what is happening.

"What is going on? Cat got your tongue?"

I laugh at her accidental wit and give her a bear hug. She is vertically challenged, so I lift her off the ground, and she yells at me to put her down. As I do, I give her a kiss on the cheek. I relinquish her from my hug and gently place her back on the floor with the delicacy she deserves. I run past her up the stairs, taking two at a time. I haven't seen my father in what feels like a lifetime and will gladly confront a tiger for any opportunity to be with him.

I reach the third floor of our family townhouse and smell my father's familiar aftershave. After he passed away, I used to go up to his room from time to time and take a deep inhalation of his favorite cardigan. I would smell a mixture of 'Joop' aftershave and Benson and Hedges cigarettes. On the night of the day he died, I sat in the garden on the spot where he had fallen and smoked two cigarettes from a pack that had been in his pocket. The plan was to create an aroma of familiarity, an unusual form of incense to provoke a mixture of emotions—remembrance and regret. After all, it was that smell that had contributed to him dying from a massive heart attack at the age of sixty-two.

My father is dead, so what form of fantasy resides in this place? Does it matter so long as I get to see him again?

I sprint along the landing and turn right into my parent's bedroom, confronted by an empty room. Light teems in through the bedroom window, highlighting the space's emptiness. I stare at the bedsheets and see a dent where he had sat.

A tear falls onto my chest and disappears. It is as if my heart is absorbing the sorrow and disappointment of not being able to see him again. I walk toward the bed but notice my reflection in the mirror on the wall to my left.

I turn and see a baby chimpanzee waving at me.

It is time to return to the jungle.

Branko is calling me back to him. I close my eyes knowing that when they open, my mother and father will be gone.

●●●

I was right. I shook my head, but the mirror was in my hand, and a monkey with weepy eyes stared back at me. I wobbled for a second due to a weakness in my legs but held a branch just in time to steady myself.

My heart was heavy, but my spirit lifted. I got to see my mother and was reminded of the need to return to my family.

But how do I return home?

I don't know where I live. I don't even know my name.

7
DANCE DANCE DANCE

I had a plan to get access to the humans. The nearest humans were those from the logging camp. Given the time that had passed, there was a chance the ugly thin man may have read my note. Even if he hadn't, I needed to win his trust. My only option was to return the lighter, as this may allow an opportunity to show him that I wasn't a normal monkey.

My only reservation was that fire had proven to be a reliable defense against attacking monkeys. Aliba and I had been much safer since our altercation with the three Hs. However, they were likely angry and embarrassed at recent events and may come looking for revenge. Giving up the lighter was a risky move, but it may have been my only option.

My desire to return to my human family put my monkey family at risk. I felt as if to be with one, I would have to sacrifice the other. Aliba was grooming me as I pondered this impossible decision. She picked through my hair and removed bits of dirt, fleas, and other foreign objects. I liked being cleaned by another, as it was both a lazy and extremely soothing experience. I felt like I was worth a million bananas after my wash, and as soon as I was clean, it was time to get dirty again. I wrestled with Mum, and we chased each other through the trees. Every day, she encouraged me to play in the canopy. I think it was her way of ensuring I developed my muscles with a good bout of grappling and got my heart going with a chase. She was an excellent P.P.E (primate physical education) teacher.

Aliba ended our play session suddenly as something spooked her. There was a shimmering noise in the trees. It sounded like the forest was closing in on us. We retreated to the nest and waited. It was as if the jungle was collapsing around us—Aliba covered my body with hers, and we hid from the approaching violent vibrations. The perimeter closed around us, and the sight of an organized army of primates suddenly surrounded us. I recognized spider monkeys, howlers, marmosets, and tamarins. They encircled us like a smothering wall of fur. Even if I had my lighter, it wouldn't have deterred that array of animals.

My monkey gibber had improved exponentially over the last few weeks, so it was time to use it to see if I could negotiate with them. I issued a warning bark, which was met with silence. One of the masses, who appeared to be the oldest primate—an ancient red howler—made a very obvious peace signal. It was two fingers shaped into a V-sign with his palm facing outward.

The aged monkey walked passively toward me with his head down and palms open. He took two steps forward and fell to his knees on the ground. All the other monkeys followed suit. The elderly primate was bright orange, but the ends of his fur were grey. I noticed the hair on top of his skull, in particular, was receding, and he had managed to comb the hair from the side of his head over and down the other side. The red howler addressed me from this crouched position with a mighty roar. *What do they want from me?* It felt like the monkey population of this jungle wanted to make me their king!

In such situations, I think letting the opposition make the first move is best. The red howler jumped up to his feet and then made a circular motion with his right hand and pointed down. The monkey ring that had surrounded us descended to the jungle floor.

Before following, I picked up the lighter from the nest. Aliba and I trailed the last of the pack and reached a cleared open square encircled by hundreds of primates. Spider monkeys hung from the rafters, tamarins in the treetops, squirrel monkeys pushed each other out of the way to get a good vantage point, and bald uakaris lurked in the mist. Only the chief howler monkey sat in the middle of the cleared space.

He beckoned me towards him, and the gathered monkey audience waited for some form of entertainment that I was central to.

The congregation was hushed and awaited the sermon, which began when the red howler began to tap his right foot. He then jumped into the air and completed a three-hundred-sixty-degree spinning lutz, which was quite remarkable given he wasn't skating on ice! The only thing more astonishing than the creature's grace was the awe inspired by the crowd. A back flip hushed their open-mouthed faces. He then leaped forward and performed a roll ending with a handstand in which he held position for five seconds before flipping onto his feet and then took a well-deserved bow.

His gymnastic excellence was met with a thunderous ovation. Inspired by the surrounding euphoric reaction, for the finale, he leaped from the ground onto a branch six feet in the air, bounced into the stratosphere, did three somersaults, and dismounted with a feather-light landing.

The gathered crowd offered heartfelt, rapturous applause. I had to agree—that was an awesome display that combined athleticism and modern dance. I joined in the applause at my host's show of dancing prowess. The red howler retreated to the far end of the inner circle and bowed. Worryingly, I now had the ominous feeling his performance was not simply a gift for me, but instead the crowd was expecting my response.

The audience started nervously chattering. Fighting broke out amongst differing troops of monkeys. I saw Handlebar lurking in the crowd, sheepishly watching me over another monkey's shoulder. A burly black howler descended from the trees and let out a deafening scream of disapproval. The attendees then fell silent. The ancient red monkey pointed at me again and stamped his right foot. It was my turn, and this wasn't the kind of primate that you wanted to disappoint.

As a human, I didn't dance unless I was relatively tipsy. Most of my best moves on the dance floor occurred when I was inebriated. Therefore, this was going to be an interesting and sobering experience. I started a hand clap that gradually increased in speed. *Boom but ta boom but taboom but ta boombuttaboom!*

I was a slightly hairier version of John Travolta; tonight was Saturday and it was feverish in the jungle. My routine began with a disco pose. Right arm pointed up at the sky, left arm pointing down at the forest floor. I span energetically to my right, but the crowd didn't seem terribly impressed.

I urgently needed to pull out the big guns, so I moved to the *Mashed Potato*. It was a great move, and suddenly, Jackie Wilson was singing in my ears. The *Swim* seemed an appropriate segue so I broke that out next. To jazz things up a bit, I did a standing breaststroke move and then backflipped. When I landed, I transitioned to a backstroke.

This crowd was tough and showed their insouciance by half-heartedly clapping their support. In my desperation to win them over, I started to dance the *Monkey*. This is where you bend your knees and put your curled arms under your armpits. This elicited even less applause, and unfortunately, I could now hear a few high-pitched laughs.

In a last-ditch attempt born out of absolute despair, it was time for the moonwalk. Due to nervous energy, it wasn't as smooth as I would have liked. I decided it was better to go down in flames than just to fade away, so my moonwalk merged into the *Macarena*, and I ended with a flip and an attempted yell of "Hey, Macarena!"

If I were in the Wild West, this would be a tumbleweed moment, and I should rightly have been shot dead. Instead, I looked back at Aliba, and she was smiling—but no one else matched her motherly enthusiasm.

I do not think it would be out of place to say my dancing had actually offended some of the crowd.

The polite members of the audience were still facing me, but many of the congregation had turned their backs on me. Unfortunately, those most annoyed had flung particles of feces in my direction. Fortuitously, they had poor aim, and I managed to avoid being struck.

With a smile, the old red howler pointed at himself. The crowd applauded, barked, cheered, and rejoiced. He then pointed at me, and a little monkey started cheering wildly. He realized he was alone in doing so and was immediately muted by embarrassment.

It appeared I had lost the democratic vote. The howker's smile turned to a solemn look, and then, slowly, he raised a finger to his throat and drew a line across it.

Had I known the outcome of th contest was that the loser was put to death, I probably wouldn't have played the game!

I reached back and picked up the lighter at my mother's feet. I raised it into the air and flicked the flint wheel. Unfortunately, the flame of protection was not forthcoming. I tried again with the same result.

It looked like Luke was going to have to do without his lightsaber. The force was certainly not with me tonight.

Being surrounded by an army of primates baying for blood was the point when most people would start to panic, and I was exactly the same as most people. I grabbed Aliba's hand and hoped for a miracle.

An act of God arrived in the form of a grateful alley! A snort sounded in the distance, the ground shook from the impact of a charging animal.

Nishpunk had decided to enter this monkey party, and he was going to make it rock and roll. Have you ever seen a bull elephant invade a monkey soiree? It was not a pretty sight. Nishpunk was more than a leveler in this battle, and he burst through the cordon, sending monkeys and tamarins flying. I saw him tread on a fleeing marmoset and fling a capuchin into the heavens. Tamarinds took flight, titi monkeys cut and ran, muriqui left, and squirrel monkeys scrammed.

The only monkeys who didn't vanish were Aliba and me, although she was extremely keen to flee. Nishpunk sidled toward us and encouraged us to hop on. We climbed onto and sat like royalty on his back. Although the monkey army disbanded rapidly, I quickly realized we were much safer with Nishpunk than without him.

The monkey collective had forced my hand. My differences from the other monkeys were too evident. My unusual behavior had made me an enemy of the clan. This jungle was no longer safe for Aliba and me. We headed in the direction of the human settlement. Right now, that was the only place we were not in immediate danger.

8
UGLY SALVATION

Nishpunk's back was surprisingly comfortable. The thick, coarse hairs that stuck out of his skin looked like bits of black wire but were unexpectedly soft. Otherwise, it was a firm and spacious bed. He had walked to safety at the edge of the forest, and we were resting in the shade a few feet from the river. It was an eventful and danger-fraught afternoon, and we all needed rest. Aliba and Nishpunk were sleeping comfortably while I watched the trees for would-be monkey assassins, though I doubted any attacker would be brave enough to approach us after Nishpunk's furious display of strength.

I noticed a bush covered in little purple dots. If I remembered correctly from Aliba's teaching, those berries were safe to eat and quite delicious. I hopped off Nishpunk's back and started collecting a snack for my companions. I loved waking up to a treat whether as a monkey or a human. Ashley used to prepare breakfast for me and bring it to me in bed. She would hand-feed me grapes or berries while I played the role of Caesar. It seemed strange that the few lucid recollections I possessed were of her. She was carefully preserved in my mind like diamond-encrusted memories in a jewelry box of emotions. Although my general recall was fragmented, her reminiscence was undiminished, and she retained perfect clarity. I remembered her love for me, which was odd when I wasn't sure who I was. I closed my eyes and ate a berry. They were not fully ripe, so they tasted slightly sour.

The small magical mirror popped into my head, and I regretted leaving it in the family nest. I had a strong desire to retrieve it, but returning to the nest would not be safe. I will have to go on a recovery mission in the next few days.

However, a journey that was infinitely more urgent was going back to the logger's hut and returning the lighter to the ugly, thin man. Aliba would be safe with Nishpunk whilst I left. I prepared a pile of berries on a layer of leaves by Nishpunk's trunk. A treat for my companions to wake up to.

My vine-swinging technique was like poetry in motion, such that without any effort, I had made it to the logging camp in no time at all. It was the middle of the afternoon, and the camp was unusually inactive. A few people walked into a hut and out again with trays of human slop. My insect, berry, and nut mix looked far more appetizing than their unidentifiable sustenance.

The coast seemed clear as the camp was so quiet. I eased myself down the tree onto the headquarter's roof. I entered the window and, sat on the ugly, thin man's desk and waited.

His desk was much cleaner than last time, so there were no stray pens to use to scribe a meaningful message. I dropped the lighter onto the desk. My tail was quite tired from carrying it! I rubbed my tail and realized how useful it was to have a tail in addition to arms! There were some obvious benefits to being a monkey. *Hopefully, the sight of the lighter will calm the ugly thin man.* I was worried about the lack of a means of communication, but I needed to make contact with a person. The human part of my soul was desperate to connect with mankind. I felt a step closer to Ashley and my family by trying to make a connection with people.

As I sat patiently, I noticed a map on the cabin's wall. It seemed to be a map of the country I was in—below the map it read, *Obrigado por visitarem o Brasil.* The map had been produced by the B.A.T, listed in brackets below as Brasiliero Agência de Turismo. I always wanted to go to Brazil. However, I never envisioned being here under these circumstances! I wondered if I was a better footballer now that I was Brazilian rather than English.

I scrunched up a piece of paper, threw it in the air, and managed two kick-ups. The paper ball bounced on the table and then fell to the floor. If it was possible, my football ability seemed to have regressed rather than improved. I jumped off the table to retrieve the piece of paper. The door opened as I hit the floor, and someone entered the room. Suddenly afraid, I decided to lie low. The desk concealed me from view. If this was the ugly thin man, perhaps he would notice the lighter? I listened intently for a reaction.

The feet walked up to the desk and stopped. I heard the rustling of paper and then silence. It sounded as if he just grabbed something on the table. A voice broke the silence, "My English is not as good as it should be. But if you are still in the room, amigo, please show yourself. I will not harm you."

As my dad used to say, *You have to speculate to accumulate.* I had to take a risk to create a better potential outcome.

I ran past the feet of the standing man and jumped onto a wooden chair in the corner of the room. The ugly, thin man turned to face me, infinitely calmer than when I first saw him, and his face was less hostile. He raised his palms and spoke quietly, "Please do not run. I will not hurt you." He reached into his back pocket, and I edged toward the window to make my escape. "Please, do not flee!"

Unsure of his motives, I had to tame the beast within and try to trust. If he was going to attack me, he would have done so already. If necessary, I needed to keep a keen eye on his movements and be ready to scarper to survive.

He placed a pack of cigarettes on the desk. From the gold carton, I knew they were Benson and Hedges. He put his hand into his back trouser pocket and pulled out his wallet. When he opened the wallet, out came a familiar piece of paper. Carefully, he unfolded it and read the familiar message, "Help."

He addressed me again in a very gentle voice, "I must be going crazy. But I need to ask you a question. I think this may be the strangest conversation of my life. I am talking with a *monkey.*" He guffawed and then regained his composure. He stared straight into my eyes and said the words I had been longing to hear, "Did you write this message?"

Houston, I have just made contact with humankind. If making fire was a massive evolutionary jump, then this was an evolutionary elevator. This was one small step for primates and one giant leap for monkeykind. I nodded my head in response to his question. The ugly thin man's face broke into a smile. His face morphed into the friendliest face imaginable. I could never imagine yellow teeth, squinting eyes, grey hair on a balding head, and an enormous nose to combine so beautifully. This was the face of salvation.

"Hello, little friend, my name is Gabriel."

9
GLORIOUS DEFENDER

I scrawled a frantic message on a piece of paper in front of me. I turned the inscribed note to face Gabriel who continued to sit patiently in front of a monkey capable of communication. He read the words out loud, "I am a boy." After he said the words, Gabriel made the sign of the cross over his chest. He grabbed a glass of water and took a slug. I imagine he wished it was something stronger. Gabriel wasn't sitting in front of a capable primate; I was the cleverest monkey in history.

"I haven't made that sign on my chest in a long time. I stopped believing God influenced my life. I never thought I would see such a vision. A monkey who can write! A monkey who thinks he is a boy."

What does he mean, thinks he is a boy? Well, it must be difficult for anyone to understand. I was just glad I knew how to write. Gabriel continued, "Tell me more, little one."

I wrote a longer message, turned the page, and waited for him to read it aloud. "I was in some sort of accident. Then I awoke in this monkey's body." Gabriel's eyes were like giant saucers. He seemed awe-struck with anticipation. "Well, this is quite astonishing. What is your name, my little friend?"

I sat and considered Gabriel's question. What was my name? I remembered my girlfriend's name, and that she was Turkish. My mother's face was clear in my mind, as was my brother's daughter. I knew my dad smoked Benson and Hedges cigarettes and owned a grey cardigan, but I couldn't remember my name.

I found writing with the pen quite difficult as my small primate hands couldn't easily manipulate the thick implement. The last message made my hand ache, and the pen dropped from my grip when I completed the sentence.

My new human friend read out the message, "I cannot remember my human name. I lived in England. Now, my name is Branko."

Gabriel looked as stunned as if someone had just told him they were a human trapped in a monkey's body! It was quite obvious he was shocked by the implications of our meeting. After all, it's not a standard day when a monkey pops into the office to become a pen pal. After a few minutes of silence, Gabriel swallowed the obstruction lodged in his throat and spoke in a hoarse mutter. "I cannot believe this. Little Branko, I think you are surely a gift from God. Do you know what Branko means? It is a very rare Slavic name. I only know this because someone very close to me was called Branko."

I could see Gabriel had tears in his eyes as he said these words. He started sobbing and lowered his gaze towards the ground. I looked left and saw a crumpled handkerchief which I grabbed and offered to him. He looked up and raised his hand to accept it. He stifled his sniffling and wiped tears from his eyes.

"Why thank you little Branko. Life is truly magical. I had stopped believing life could be that way." He paused again to sob into the handkerchief. "I am sorry Branko, this afternoon is very unexpected. However, you must know why the name Branko is so important to me.

"A long time ago, I was married. My wife was a beautiful woman called Angelica. Many years ago, I lived in Austria, in Vienna. In my former life, I studied literature at the University Wien. My German is far better than my English! Each lunchtime, I would go to the same cafe in Vienna. I would sit and order the same meal. I was extremely lonely in that city. I found it very difficult to make friends and spent much of my time alone. Then, one day, in that cafe, she appeared. The stunning and radiant Angelica walked up and asked me for my order. I continued to go to the cafe each day. I started writing poetry about her but was too afraid to speak to her. However, one day, when she approached to ask for my order, she asked me what I was writing. I froze! Not wanting to seem like a complete madman, I pushed the sheet of paper to her. The poem was about her. I remember every word:

I am alone in a city of strangers,
sinking into the concrete sand,
drowning in a river of desolation,
but you are my redemption,
your walk to my table is a crescendo,
your arrival in my life is my salvation,
can basking in your presence satisfy me?
To kiss your lips would satiate my soul.

Fortunately, she was not horrified by my poetry! She might have been afraid of my inner thoughts. However, after reading the poem, she reached over the table and grabbed my hand. Our love was a whirlwind, and she reciprocated my devotion. We were married within six months, and I truly believed life was wonderful. But, the end of this perfect chapter in my life was due to a Branko…"

I was shocked. How could my name have such significance to Gabriel? He slammed his fist on the table, and I jumped back in shock. I overcame a strong desire to escape as I knew that I had to hear this story and was confident Gabriel would not hurt me.

Seeing the panic on my face, Gabriel sought to alleviate my worry, "I am sorry, Branko! I am not angry with you, but it has been so long since I have considered these emotions. I was desperate to have children, and so was Angelica. I prayed to the Lord every night that I would have a boy. Angelica laughed because I wanted a boy so much. She asked me if I would love a daughter with the same intensity. I asked her how she thought I could not adore a daughter if that child resembled her. She said if she created a boy, then she had one wish, that he should be named after her father."

Gabriel paused again. His speech became panicked and was broken intermittently by sobbing. I hoped he wouldn't lash out again.

"There were complications in the pregnancy. In her seventh month, she felt sharp pains in her stomach. She started bleeding very heavily. We rushed her to hospital, but the doctors told us she would have to give birth prematurely."

Gabriel paused and lowered his eyes. They were filled with an ocean of tears, which began raining down his large nose. He silently wept whilst I sat and waited, knowing exactly how the story would end.

"She believed the name was an omen. That her father was successful in life and that her son should be called the same. My little boy was born two months prematurely. He survived for five hours and fifteen minutes, but his birthday and his day of death were the same: October 29th. Angelica had already perished from the exertions of trying to deliver him. I told him his name meant *glorious defender* but wondered why he could not defend his mother. I watched my son take his last breath shortly after seeing my wife take hers. I whispered his name over and over again. Please don't leave me alone. My poor little boy. My glorious defender. My Branko."

I always wondered how similar monkeys are to humans. Well, monkeys can cry, too. As man and monkey wept together, I recalled that October 29th was my birthday in my previous life.

iO
i DREAM OF BUDDHA

When the fat man entered the cabin, he saw a rather unusual sight. Gabriel had always been a tough boss at the logging camp, so seeing him weeping by his desk and then noticing a crying monkey on the table must have been a shock.

Gabriel was wiping his eyes as the chunky chap lunged in my direction. Fortunately, the large man was clumsy, and I had my wits about me, so I was out the window before he could strike. Gabriel screamed with rage at the obese oik but couldn't prevent him from chasing me out of the cabin. I decided it might be sensible to rest on the roof. It was at that moment I felt a sharp pain in my side. I looked to my left side and saw a metal dart with a bright pink fluffy tail end. The material looked like candyfloss. *Where did this dart come from? I suppose I will solve that mystery after a little snooze…* Suddenly, I was very sleepy. *I just needed a moment's rest, and then I will tell off the culprit firing darts around. You could have a monkey's eye out with such an object—*

● ● ●

I awoke from my slumber almost immediately. I look up at the canopy of trees surrounding me. To my amazement, I see the familiar sparkling light reflecting in the distance. Climbing isn't required, as I fly straight up to the light and am level with it in a second. It is the mirror I left in my nest. I look inside the mirror, but my reflection doesn't shine back.

Instead, I see a man sitting at a table. As I peer closer to try and identify the man, my head feels top heavy and imbalanced as it approaches the mirror. The weight of my head eases me toward the reflective glass, which grows in size before my very eyes. Either the mirror was growing to accommodate me, or am I shrinking? The mirror is now larger than my body, and I can see the man more clearly.

He waves at me, encouraging me to approach. He is wearing an orange toga, and I am certain I recognise that face. My emotions overwhelm me, and I jump through the looking glass without a second thought.

Gravity reverts to normal, and I walk up to a table that separates the man from me. On the table surface is a pack of cards spread out as a fan. I stare up from the cards and am amazed at who sits in the yoga position before me—partially due to the dexterity of the fellow but more so due to their relationship to me.

We are in a small square room. My half of the room is green and appears to have a leaf pattern drawn onto the walls. The other half is painted in a brilliant white—so bright that looking directly at the dazzling color is slightly painful, like when you glance at the sun.

As I approach the man, I am sure of his identity. The familiar face is my middle brother!

He is wearing orange robes similar to those of a Buddhist monk and a beige headdress. He is sitting in the lotus position and smiling broadly. I address him by raising my arms and stepping around the table to embrace him. As I do, I collide with a transparent barrier. I fall back to the floor and rub my nose.

He shakes his head, and I can see him mouth the word, "dumbass."

This is definitely my brother, as *dumbass* was his affectionate nickname for me in my former life. I look through the glass and notice his hand on a button on the table. He presses it and speaks. His voice echoes around my side of the room, although I can't see any evidence of a speaker system.

"Hello, little brother! How are you doing? Apologies for the invisible, impenetrable glass wall, but I don't think you can be on this side of the division. So, best to stick to your side. Take a seat and then take a card."

His voice seems to emanate from every inch of my surroundings. It is not deafening, but it is commanding enough that I take a seat promptly. I see an equivalent red button on the table before me and press it down, "What happened to me?"

"Pick a card?" My brother had an annoying habit of answering a question with another question when we were children. He did this to me as a youngster to help me figure stuff out for myself. I selected a card and turned it upward to reveal a joker.

My brother pressed the red button and said, "The joker means you aren't taking this experience seriously. To be honest, that is consistent with your general approach when you were human. I have another question for you. Who am I?"

The embarrassment of not knowing your brother's name was not an enjoyable feeling, and it reminded me of how lost I was and how desperately I needed my brother's help. "Well, I know your name, brother, but I need you to know mine. Rather than seeking to trick me, can you help for a change?"

He isn't easily fooled and retorts, "Go on then, tell me my name. I don't think you can remember. What a disgrace, you not remembering your brother's name! Do you recall the time I beat up the boys bullying you at school? Remember the time I taught you how to fight for yourself? Well, I can't always be there to protect you. You are in a lot of trouble right now and need to help yourself. There isn't anyone to protect you where you are, and I don't think you want to remember. So, pull yourself together and tell me my name."

I am embarrassed in a way that only my brother could make me, as he has unearthed my shameful secret. I have never given in to my older brother's bullying tactics, so I verbally procrastinate, delaying the inevitable. "How could I not know your name? I know our older brother's name. I know my girlfriend's name. I know my niece's name. You are even giving me a hint with the clothing you are wearing."

My anonymous brother smiled with appreciation for me, recognizing this hint. "Yes, little brother, I am."

Immediately, I remember another segment of the past. My parents were devout Buddhists. My father used to tell me fables about the Lord Buddha when I was a child. As he was tucking me into bed, he would ask me if I would like to hear a magical story. My Dad spoke with such pride when he regaled me with stories about Buddha, always mindful of reminding me he was a man and not a God. As a child, I considered Buddha a superhero rather than a religious figure. He was born in a place called Lumbini as a prince named Siddhartha. He spent twenty-nine years as a prince but never felt comfortable with his wealth and material possessions.

Rather than live as a prince and then a king, Siddhartha fled from his royal responsibility to become a mendicant. After living as a beggar on the streets, he started his religious studies to reach enlightenment.

His path to sophisticated awareness happened through near-total deprivation of worldly goods, including food, through a practice called *self-mortification*. After nearly starving himself to death by restricting his food intake to only a leaf or nut per day, he collapsed in a river while bathing and almost drowned.

Siddhartha reconsidered his path after this near-death experience. Rather than complete self-deprivation, Siddhartha followed the *Middle Way*, meaning he ate only enough to survive and meditate.

Right before an extended meditation session, he ate a little milk and rice pudding he received from a young girl and then rested under a Bodhi tree in Bodh Gaya in India. He decided to rest at this spot and meditate until enlightenment. He rested under the Bodhi tree for forty-nine days and achieved enlightenment at age thirty-five. At the summit of human perception, he was believed to have realized a complete awakening and insight into the nature and cause of human suffering, which was ignorance, along with the steps necessary to eliminate it.

Upon reaching enlightenment, Siddhartha became the Lord Buddha, a bit like how Peter Parker became Spiderman. He'd progressed from being a normal human to becoming something more. My father named my brother Sidath after the Buddha or 'The Enlightened One.'

After an extended deliberation mulling over my father's bedtime stories, I announce triumphantly, "Your name is Sidath."

"Well, that took a while, didn't it! What else did the story tell you?"

"The story is about how the Lord Buddha became enlightened. How did you know what I was thinking about?"

"Look, little brother. This is a journey for which you must start to take some responsibility. However, I will give you a clue. Sometimes, a boy must leave his comfortable environment to become something else. That change may be necessary for the boy's survival, or it might destroy him. Why are you here as Branko? Who were you before? I know you know my name, but what is yours?"

I open my mouth to respond but can not get the words out. I try to inhale but there is no air in the room. My brother waves at me and removes the yellow headdress. He looks back towards me and points to a black hole puncturing the room's green side. The air is siphoned out of it. I spin round and round, being sucked out of the room along with the air like water spiraling down a sink.

●●●

I found myself slumped face down on a hard, cold, wooden floor. The room was dark, but some light shone from the edge of a door frame in front of me. I tried to stand, and my head hit a hard ceiling. I fell immediately to the ground and reached forward. My hand hit a solid wooden bar about two inches thick. I moved my hand across, and it met another bar. Rather than stand, I sat back on my bottom and felt around me.

A hard, square wooden cage surrounded me at arm's width. The enclosed area was high enough for me to sit upright but not much bigger.

I was trapped in a forest in Brazil. I was trapped in a prison cell. I was trapped in the body of a monkey.

ii
NELSON'S LESSONS

B eing caged was contrary to my natural instincts as a human and a monkey. I found this situation mentally as well as physically claustrophobic. The wooden cage floor was cold, and so was my heart. I felt as if the optimism of the past weeks had been sucked out of me. No matter what progress I made, circumstances kept obstructing me. Two steps forward, and then I got shot by a tranquilizer dart and placed in a cage. The real dampener on my spirits was the darkness in my mind. I was alone and afraid. Where could I turn for inspiration? I barely remembered my family or my girlfriend. My friends in this jungle had abandoned me.

A quote popped into my head. "I learned courage was not the absence of fear, but the triumph over it. The brave man is not he who does not feel afraid, but he who conquers that fear." It was not cowardly to feel fear. The brave man can conquer it. Only a wise man who had vanquished his demons could make such a statement. *Nelson Mandela, I wish you would open that door and take me on a long walk to freedom!*

The reminiscence of Mandela took me back to my childhood. I was sitting in the front passenger seat of my father's car. It was a warm summer's day, the twenty-eighth of June 1989, and my father and I were driving in London. The open windows and sunroof were allowing glorious sunshine to fill the car. It was Nelson Mandela's birthday, and we were protesting for his release from imprisonment. We shouted in unison, "Free Nelson MANDELA! Free Nelson MANDELA! Free Nelson MANDELA!" This went on and on until our voices were hoarse. My dad looked at me and said to shout so Nelson could hear me in

South Africa because he would be lonely in his cell on his birthday. I started chanting again, "Free Nelson MANDELA!"

The memory faded, and I was back in my cage. So, I yelled in monkey gibber: "Free Nelson MANDELA!" I felt empowered by this chant. I felt as strong as a bear. They could jail my body, but they could not confine my mind, and I was not afraid. *When I see an opportunity, I will escape and return to Nishpunk and Aliba. Then I will explain to them, as best I can, that I have to go away. I will entrust myself to Gabriel and ask for his help to return to England. If I can get closer to my family, I might remember where I live in London.*

First, I have to get out of this cage.

As I considered escape, the door to the hut burst open, but Nelson Mandela was not standing in the sunlight. The light shining in my eyes prevented me from identifying the visitor. He had a dog on a leash—a large snarling Alsatian—and it was straining to come at me. It was jerking against the restrained grip of the owner. My pupils adjusted to see the stout man standing before me.

"Hello, little monkey," he began. "You nearly got away. Lucky that dart hit you in the side. Don't want you running around the forest when I can get a pretty penny for you from the local docs. Are you scared in there? Don't worry. Bruno won't eat you. I won't let him. He don't get to eat something so precious as you."

I recognized this bloke's dialect and was sure the well-fed gentleman had a British accent. It was strange to hear such a voice again after what had seemed an eternity. I began to wonder what happened to Gabriel. Why hadn't he come to my rescue? Perhaps he had been prevented by this brute?

Bruno came up to the cage and bared his large canines with a salivating snarl. His breath smelt like dog food, gingivitis, and death. He seemed to be an experienced primate murderer. He may be man's best friend, but certainly wasn't monkey's!

The bulky man yanked Bruno's chain and pulled him out of the room. My recent lack of fear and Mandela-inspired confidence followed Bruno out the door.

What now? Unfortunately, I left my rampaging elephant with my mother in the forest hours ago. They might not even be there when I get back. I needed to hope that Gabriel could free me from this situation. I was sure he would be looking for me. There was a link between us that couldn't be broken. Something brought Branko and me to him. It cannot be a coincidence that his son passed away the day I was born and shared the name Branko. Gabriel was an older man, probably in his mid to late fifties. I was born as a human about twenty years ago.

Could it be that I was his son in a former life? I really was losing the plot and a grasp of reality, but perhaps I was his Branko before living my last life?

Reincarnation was a possibility. What else could explain my being a human before and now a monkey? Was fate playing a game on us both? Was the spirit of his child lost in this jungle, and was he the only person who could help me now? So many questions. I wasn't a good Buddhist in my last life, and this was the consequence. Karma was mocking the boy who turned into a monkey. That seemed to be the only rational explanation in this confused reality. In reincarnation, the soul was not supposed to retain memory from a previous life, so why could I remember parts of who I was?

The hut door creaked open, and I hoped that the smelly dog wouldn't come back without fat male supervision. In place of Bruno stood a pretty middle-aged woman with short blond hair and a warm smile. She edged toward me whilst cautiously peering with squinted eyes at my cage. It appeared she was wearing a white bib, and I think she had a stethoscope around her neck. Was this one of the doctors the fat man mentioned? I retreated to the back of the cage. The woman noticed my apprehension and sat on the same level as the wooden box.

"Please don't be afraid, Branko. Gabriel sent me."

12
FALLEN CHAMPION

L ook, you will have to do something to prove you are a monkey of superior intelligence," said the woman. "I know Gabriel is convinced, but I am the one pulling the jailbreak, so can you do something... I don't know... *spectacular?*"

I was somewhat bemused. My would-be savior would only free me from this cage if I took on the role of a performing chimpanzee. I didn't know what spectacular thing I could do inside a wooden cage, so I waved at her.

"Look, Branko, you are going to have to do better than that. Okay, let's play Simon says. Simon says rub your head."

I mimicked her movement.

"Okay, this is looking good. Simon says rub your belly." I did as she asked, and she responded with a deep sigh of amazement. I took a deep breath, then raised my index finger to my head, pointed at my temple, and slowly rotated my finger. The universal sign of crazy.

My would-be savior laughed out loud and then remembered why she was performing sign language with a monkey. She whispered, "Oh, very funny, Branko! Sorry, I had to be sure. I will try and get you out of there immediately."

She got off the floor and walked towards the cage but tripped on something. She staggered and fell in my direction. I cowered with my eyes shut, but when I opened my eyes, I realized, fortunately, she had fallen to the side of my cage. This woman was not my ideal rescuer, but I wasn't in a position to be picky! Her smiling face was now inches from my cage.

"Oopsie Daisy, well, now I am down at your height. Look at what I have found." She reached to the top of the cage and picked up a set of keys, which she

THE BOY IN THE MONKEY

dangled in front of me. She unlocked the cage door and pulled it open. I stepped out and raised my hand to hers. She shook it and said, "Hello, Branko, my name is Christa." I then jumped up her body and gave her a huge hug. She was taken aback but hugged me back gently. Christa spoke with an American accent, likely from an international education. "Okay, little one, we haven't got any time to waste. You stay under my shirt and hold on tight. I'll get you to Gabriel. Now, stay hidden and be quiet. No one can see you in there."

I climbed round to Christa's back, holding onto her under t-shirt. Her overshirt loosely covered me. My clenched grip held the neck of her tee and belt.

Riding on her back in the dark reminded me of being in the boot of my school friend's car! If we had too many people to fit in the car, we drew straws to see who went in the boot. The most terrifying part of riding in the boot of a car was the paranoia of potentially being rear-ended and crushed by another vehicle. Being stuck in traffic meant you could hear the engine of the car next to you. I hated being in the boot, but we were boys, and those were the games we played. *How come I can remember useless information like that and not my name?*

Christa exited the hut, and I could feel the sunshine warming me through her shirt. My body was quite stiff and sore due to the combination of being tranquilized and then confined to a cage. I hadn't eaten a meal since the berries of the morning long ago. My mind drifted to Aliba and the worry she must be experiencing. I have been away for over half the day, and I am sure she will have waited in that same spot for my return. She would never leave me. I have to see Gabriel and then return to her. The sound of a dog barking ended my daydreaming. Christa's pace slowed. I could hear footsteps walking in the gravel toward us, and the barking was getting more frequent, louder, and more agitated.

Christa whispered, "Keep out of sight, Branko. Huggins is coming over to us." The steps of the approaching Huggins stopped, and I heard Bruno's unmistakable whining. He was pulling at his master Huggins's leash, desperate to investigate the familiar smell of monkey on Christa.

"Aw right, Christa," said Huggins. "You're looking pretty hot today, I mean, for an older chick. Bruno, what the 'ell are you doing? Stop getting at the lady, or I'll smack ya."

"I suppose I should be grateful for the compliment," Christa replied calmly. "You British are such gentlemen. What is wrong with your dog, Huggins? Please try and keep him under control."

Bruno's whining became more desperate and his barking more aggressive. I felt like I was in the back of a car boot, and the engine in the car behind was revving up and ready to smash into me.

"Did you eat sausages this morning?" Huggins responded. "He goes a bit wild at the smell of sausages. Maybe that's it. Maybe you could come round to my cabin for sausages sometime?" Huggins laughed and let out a sordid chuckle. I was sure Christa and I were united in our dislike for him.

"I can't decide what would be worse," Christa replied. "The meal or the company. Also, Huggins, you should think about some vegetables in your diet. You look like you are six months pregnant!"

I made a mistake and giggled at this comment. It was a very slight whisper of a laugh, but Bruno must have approached Christa because she took a sudden step back.

"What the 'ell is wrong with you Bruno?" screamed Huggins. "Right, 'ave that!"

I heard the dog yelp, and then Huggins's feet shuffled away as he dragged Bruno away from Christa. "Damn dog, no sausages for you tonight. Can't control yourself when I am speaking to a lady."

Christa whispered to me again, "Okay, Bruno, they're leaving. That was far too close for comfort. The dog wanted minced monkey for dinner. We are not far from Gabriel. Be calm and stay low."

I patted her back with my fingers as she continued walking for about thirty seconds. I heard a door open and was suddenly overcome by a familiar smell. The odor was instantly recognizable to anyone who had been in a hospital. I hated that smell. It always reminded me of seeing my dad unwell in a hospital bed. He survived three heart attacks when I was a child, but his demise was inevitable due to how weak each coronary made him.

The memory that had sunk deepest into my mind, the one that cannot be stripped away even when reincarnated as a monkey, was Christmas when I was seven years old...

●●●

I enter the hospital surrounded by my brothers and an auntie and uncle who had been looking after us. All of us are choked up with emotion as we walk up the steps of St. George's Hospital. We see the signs for different departments and follow the red lettering stating *Cardiac Ward.*

My oldest brother, Amal, tells me to smile and not let Dad know I'm sad. I know I have to be strong otherwise I might upset him, and he could get sicker. I don't understand what a triple heart bypass is, but I can tell it is a grave situation. Because of it, I had not seen my dad for a week. I had barely seen my mother either until we were moved into my uncle's house. I was excited to see my dad but now I worry about how unwell he will be.

The lift stops, and as we exit the elevator; I can already feel tears welling in my eyes. I walk out into the corridor, my uncle and auntie in front and my brothers beside me. As we enter the ward, I can hear monitors beeping, old men coughing, and the shuffling of nurses' feet. The smell overwhelms me—it is of disinfectant combined with human-produced fluids. No matter what cleaner you use, you can't wash away the smell of dried blood, urine, vomit, and feces.

The crowd parts, and my uncle and auntie step aside. My brothers step back and give me a causeway. My mum is ahead of me. Her eyes are red, and she looks tired. I run to her and give her a hug. She squeezed me back. I wish I could remain in that grasp forever. It is so much more comforting than having to see my father in that bed.

She can tell I am reluctant to look at him, so she whispers to me. "Now, Appa is very weak, so you mustn't grab at him. He has had an operation but is recovering. He wanted to see you, so go over and give him a kiss and rub his hand. Be careful of the wires though. Okay?"

I do not reply, and instead reluctantly turn to my father lying in the bed.

His eyes are half open and I am not sure if he is awake or asleep. I was struck by how frail and thin he looked.

What happened to my grizzly Dad capable of bear-hugs?

I see the scar tissue and stitches running from the middle of his chest down to his stomach. Then I see the wires attached to his chest running to monitors, creating inconsistent beeps. Blood runs from plastic bags down into tubes in his arms. My champion had fallen.

I look back at my mother, uncertain of what to do. I glance across at my brothers, and they had pensive expressions. I am not sure of the right thing to do. When I returned my gaze to my father, he is looking at me.

His head remains still on the pillow. I think he is trying trying to minimize movement, but he gestures with his finger for me to approach.

I walk over slowly and hold his hand. He tried to squeeze, but his grip is so soft and far weaker than mine. His hands have always felt delicate, but this time, they feel fragile, like old silk.

I climb on a chair beside the bed and lean in to kiss him on the cheek. He sees me coming and turns his head, puckered at the same time, and gives me a kiss. I see a tear in his eye. I probably have one in mine, too.

●●●

As Christa came to a halt, I was brought back to reality in what I believed was some kind of hospital ward. I heard Gabriel's voice, "Have you got him?"

Christa replied, "Branko, it is safe to come out." I escaped from under Christa's t-shirt and climbed around onto her shoulder. She was standing at the foot of Gabriel's bed. We were in a makeshift infirmary ward. There were three beds in a sorry-looking wooden cabin. Gabriel sat in the bed furthermost to the right. He appeared extremely weary and was incapable of raising himself from the bed.

"Hello, Branko, my boy!" Gabriel exclaimed warmly. "I am so sorry I couldn't come and get you myself, but I had a slight episode."

"That episode is known as a *heart attack*," Christa interrupted.

I couldn't believe my actions had led to Gabriel being in hospital. I jumped off Christa onto the bed and rubbed Gabriel's hand. Gabriel sensed my guilt and sought to console me, "Don't worry, little one. This is not your fault. I have spent a lifetime feeling numb and living without emotion. The happiness I felt when you came into my life has rejuvenated me! However, perhaps such a sudden jolt of happiness is too great for anyone. It seems my heart could not take the strain!" I hugged Gabriel's arm, and suddenly, I was a seven-year-old boy again. Gabriel handed me a pen and some paper from the side table.

"Branko, start writing all the information you know about your family. The magic of the internet means we might be able to track someone down." Although this was a great idea, even I knew, without any surnames, I had no escape from this monkey puzzle.

13
CHOCOLATE MONKEY

I cannot remember anyone's surnames, but my memory is coming back to me." Gabriel read my message out loud and then rubbed his stubbled chin with the back of his hand whilst cogitating. "Well, this is good. In time, you will remember more information, and if you remember your surname, we can track down your family."

The word family echoed around the room. I hoped my family in England were safe and well, but what about my family in the jungle? I have been away from Aliba and Nishpunk for the whole day.

"I must return to the jungle to check on my family." Gabriel nodded as he read the message.

"The confusing world you live in, Branko. The responsibilities of a boy and a monkey. Go to them, but come back soon. We need to figure out a way for you to return home."

I reluctantly left Gabriel and Christa. They have sacrificed a lot for me already, but I would not be able to go with a clear conscience if Aliba and Nishpunk were not safe. So, I hopped next to Christa and gently nuzzled her arm. I needed to return to Aliba and explain why I have been away. Then, I had to try to unravel an explanation for my leaving her. How could I tell my primate mother I am leaving her to return to my other family, my human family? This will test my basic grasp of monkey language to the limit! I knew the word for banana, but it can only be used in so many contexts.

I will find the words. My bond with my human family is so strong in my mind, but Aliba is why I am alive. I could sense Branko's angst at the upcoming events. I think we understood what needed to be done. However, knowing you are about to tread a difficult path does not make it any easier. Branko saved me for a reason, and it wasn't to remain in this jungle with him. My fate is to return to my human family, and Branko is coming along for the ride. I was off the bed and through a window onto the roof within seconds. I needed to be fast as Gabriel was still looking unwell.

On the roof of the infirmary hut, I spied my old friends Huggins and Bruno walking toward the mess hall. Bruno noticed me and started yelping and tugging at his lead. He received a swift and painful backhand swipe from Huggins.

I snickered at his misfortune as I bounded over the rooftops until I reached Gabriel's hut. I flew up through the trees and was at the rickety bridge within moments. I prayed Nishpunk and Aliba have remained at the same spot downriver. I approached the area where I had left them resting, and they were not obviously present. However, it appeared their pile of berries had gone, so at least they had eaten. I walked to the clearing in the trees, where I left them sleeping, and stepped into some red liquid in a small pool on the ground. At first, I assumed it was the remnants of the berries after someone had gorged themselves, but I quickly realized berry juice was not so viscous. This liquid was thick, sticky, and concentrated. What was this red stuff, and why was my heart racing?

Don't panic. It could be anything.

I spun, looking for evidence of where my mother and elephant friend might be. I saw another small puddle of red liquid in a sea of dirt and leaves. I ran, following the direction of the droplets that led me to an unavoidable tragedy. My pace quickened through the trees, and terror engulfed my heart. I had been there before, when I returned home to a catastrophe, to my own personal nightmare.

I looked frantically around the flora, searching for bloody remnants, and then I saw three brown chocolate-like fingers on the forest floor. *How can there be chocolate fingers on the ground?* I walked up to the bush, concealing the remainder of the body, and touched the outer skin of the exposed fingers. Just three chocolate fingers sticking out from under a bush. I rubbed them and realized they weren't edible. They weren't moving either. I pushed the leaves of the bush back and saw the battered body of Aliba.

The bile in my stomach uncontrollably rose into my mouth. I turned my head to the side and vomited. Falling to my knees, I closed my eyes and realized I had failed another family member. *Why am I living this nightmare twice?* My head spun like a carousel. The surrounding environment lost its shape, and colors began to merge into one. Green plants, brown dirt, yellow sun, red blood, black and blue bodies, smashed faces, broken arms, dead mothers.

My eyes closed, my feet felt like they were off the floor, and my mind spiraled around my mother's corpse. I was likely to puke again at any moment, but then the mind spiral desisted. I settled onto the ground, and my feet touched the floor. I didn't want to look at Aliba's body again, but I opened my eyes desperately hoping to see a miraculously living mother monkey. Instead, my renewed vision encountered a miracle of sorts. The front door of my London family home stood before me. However, I knew this commencement was not a story with a happy ending. This memory was the only possible corner of my mind, more appalling than the present.

I smelled death in the air, and the powers that be wanted me to inhale. I saw the door and took a deep breath, readying myself for a descent into madness. I lowered my hand and took the door key from my pocket. I raised my hand to the keyhole and opened the lock to the worst horror I have ever experienced.

14
RELIVING NIGHTMARES

As I open the door, my cousin runs toward me. The words I hear from this nameless Sri Lankan relative is that my father has fallen over.

My first thought is, *Perhaps it is not so bad. Perhaps he has tripped over, sprained an ankle, or grazed his knee*, but I know no one is getting off that lightly. I sprint through the hallway of my house, past the living room, and into the garden. Already, I hear screaming. I follow my mother's frantic, high-pitched screams to the garden. I see my brother first. Dressed as lord Buddha, Sidath is crying uncontrollably into the cordless telephone. The first time we did this dance, he wasn't wearing orange robes. My mind is definitely playing tricks on me.

Sidath is speaking to the emergency services. I enter the garden and see my mother crying over my father's body. I see his still, lifeless eyes. He is dead. I know this already. I knew this the moment I saw him. His aura used to shine brightly such that his life force was magnetic. Suddenly, it is incontrovertible that he no longer exists in this world.

There is another unusual oddity altering this playback of this recollection. I can hear a song playing very quietly. It is as if the volume is ever so slightly turned up. I don't recall music playing when I first trod this path, but watching events occur again, there is an unmistakable familiar tune whispering a secret meaning.

Sidath tells me to go and see if the doctor across the road is in. I ask briefly how long my father has been down. My brother and mother are unsure. As I run out the door, I question why no one is doing CPR. Running across the road, I remember I know CPR. I must be in a very small population of monkeys who know cardiopulmonary resuscitation! The doctor across the road is not in. I stop, look up and down the road. My father is dead. How do I continue? Perhaps this is true, but I know CPR and miracles do happen. He is dead, but I must not let my brother and mother know. There is nothing I can do. I can't change the past. Why do I have to relive it?

I run back into the house. A minute has passed, but it seems like a decade. I race past crying cousins who are doing nothing useful. I gently move my mother out of the way to assess my father. Still no ambulance crew. I kneel over my hero's fallen body. His pupils are dilated. I want to close his eyelids, but it is too final a gesture. I know he has been gone for at least two minutes. Dilated pupils mean brain damage. I hope my family are unaware of this.

I check my father's pulse. There is nothing. My brother asks me if I can feel anything. I look at his crying face and tell him, "It is very faint." My father's dentures have been taken out of his mouth. I know I must try mouth-to-mouth and compressions on his heart. I have not done resuscitation in many years, and the last time was in a first aid class on a doll called Annie. I pray in my mind, let this be the moment divine intervention happens. If there is a God, then do not take my father away from me now. Let my breath bring him back to life. Let the oxygen in my lungs revive him. The strange thing is that Buddhists do not believe in a deity, and yet I find myself praying to an unknown higher power.

I hear the same song from earlier, faintly echoing through my ears. Although I can't identify the lyrics or the beat, I know the song is reminiscent of my father and our past together. The song distracts me for a moment, but I refocus on the task at hand.

I look at my father's lifeless body. I kneel next to his face and ensure no gap between his lips and mine. I blow air into his lungs. It goes in, but his chest contracts and blows the air back out. That has to be a good sign. At least there is no blockage in his airway. Okay, another breath and then ten compressions to his heart. I close the gap between my father's mouth and mine. I blow again. He produces a sound like an accordion. As the air comes out of his body, he gives off a faint whining noise. The compressions are one hand down and just left of the center of his chest. When I learned CPR at school, I always had the morbid thought that the first time I would use it would be on my father. Was that a premonition, an educated guess, or terrible luck? Probably, all three.

I compress ten times on my father's chest. "Come on, old man, you have a long way to go yet," I say this to appease my surrounding family. I do not believe the words, as I know my father has departed. I breathe twice into his mouth. He makes the same accordion imitation. Air seems to be gathering in his stomach. This is relayed to an emergency operator on the phone, and she informs me that I am probably blowing too hard. I press down on my father's stomach. The excess air escapes out of his backside. The old bugger is farting as I am trying to save his life! This is a thought I have replayed many times in my mind, and in hindsight, it is amusing. Unfortunately, at that moment, I didn't think so.

He was always terribly entertaining, but I don't think I told him so, in the way that children withhold laughter when their parents try to amuse them. His timing and manners go hand in hand. He saved the last gag for the time of his death on the patio floor in our family garden.

Now, in between compressions and breaths, I speak to the old man. Initially, it was a reassuring gesture to the disconsolate family around me. Now, I am beginning to believe the hype. "Come on, old man, you have a long way to go yet! Wake up, just keep going for a couple more minutes until the paramedics get here!"

The first paramedic comes through the door. He is unpacking his bag. Out come the epinephrine, pulse monitor, and shock pads. I move out of his way. Now is the first moment I look around and truly see the carnage of this reality. The paramedic looks at me; I dread what he will ask. "Are you comfortable to continue CPR?"

Of course, I am not. I cannot think of anything worse.

My answer was, "Yes, that is fine." He cuts the jumper and shirt from my father's upper body. Wearing a jumper on a hot day like today? That is because of his poor circulation. It is a hot, sweaty evening. The paramedic injects the epinephrine and attaches the pulse monitor.

A miracle may have occurred as there is a pulse! I ask the paramedic. He tells me it is slight. I start crying. As I compress my father's chest ten times, tears start falling from my eyes onto his chest. I hope they will help him. Perhaps my tears contain some unknown power to mend his broken body.

The paramedic tells me he will have to shock my father to get his heart going. His heart is barely beating. I look up to my left. Our neighbor is watching me. She shouts from her window, "Do you want me to come and take over?"

I look at her, and my mind says, *Yes, please take over.* Every moment is torture. I feel as if my heart is about to break. My answer is, "No, I am fine."

The paramedic shocks my father. I look at the pulse monitor. There does not seem to be a reading. "Clear," he shocks him again. I know it is all over. My brother and mother stand behind me. They are still in prayer mode. Another two paramedics run in with a stretcher and more equipment. The good thing is I can stop administering CPR as these trained professionals take over. However, I already know it will make no difference. The old boy could have a team of the world's greatest doctors around him, but it seems this is his moment. The new team administer another dose of epinephrine. I am convinced this is for show, as their body language tells a different story. It is over. We plead with them to try whatever they can, but they have done their best. He needs a new heart. I believe only a doctor can pronounce a patient as deceased, so the ambulance crew will continue this charade until relieved.

I look back to the team around my dad, who has moved him to a stretcher. They begin to wheel his body away. I tell my brother and mother to go straight to the hospital. I will go ahead with the ambulance. I know a chapter of my life has ended, but I cannot comprehend that a new chapter has already begun. I am stunned and mute as I process this truth while heading toward the ambulance.

I follow the stretcher out of the house. It is proving very difficult to move it through the narrow corridors of our ground floor. Eventually, the three paramedics loaded the body into the back of the ambulance. My consciousness has sunk deep into my mind. The visions before me are so unfamiliar that it is like a foreign language movie. Words have become indiscernible. I know everyone around me is speaking English, but I never imagined my mother saying something like, "Please God, let him live!" about my father. My brain cannot fathom the magnitude of the events. The only thing I can liken this to is watching the world end. Can this be real? How can this experience be so vivid in my mind? I thought it happened years ago.

The soundtrack to this abstract reality replays the strangely familiar chorus. I believe my memory has always had an acute affinity for sound. A song can take me back in such a way that I taste the memory and feel it, so I live that exact moment again on hearing those specific notes. I believe the phenomenon is called synaesthesia, and different humans (or monkeys) experience it in unique and subjective ways.

The ambulance begins its funeral march. Tears are running down my face. During the drive, my mood alters from calm to unbearable, frantic sobbing. I am seated beside the driver, who rubs my knee, consoling me. I take a few deep breaths to steady myself. My brain is racing so fast. Dad is gone. *You must understand this. He is not coming back.* I look over my shoulder. The other paramedic is only using one arm to continue chest compressions. His actions confirm my worst fears. At this point, I hear the siren for the first time. We are traveling fast, but it is not breakneck. Now I realize the driver knows the undeniable end as well.

"What more can be done by the doctors at the hospital?"

"The doctors will have a look at your dad and try to revive him."

"I understand, but what more can they do? You tried epinephrine. It didn't have an effect. There is not much more they can do, is there?"

The driver pauses.

"There is not much more to be done, but let's get your dad there."

I sense a lack of movement from the back of the ambulance. I look back at the other paramedic, who has stopped doing chest compressions. He unenthusiastically goes through the motions on my father's chest. I turn my head fully to look at him. He better keep going. It is not within the remit of his employment to decide when to give up on my dad. It is not within my remit either. *I will never give up on you.*

I look to my left and see something very different from the first time I experienced this memory. I am astonished to see Branko is sitting there. I am extremely glad to see him beside me. He rubs his head against my shoulder and holds my left hand. He is weeping at the loss of my father.

Looks like this time, I have a friend accompanying me on this desolate journey. I remove my hand from Branko's grip and put my left arm around my little monkey brother. He is a warm and reassuring presence. I wrap my arm around his waist and pull him close to me.

I take a last look back at my father. My throat becomes tight. I find it difficult to swallow. A chill runs down my spine. The saddest thing about death is these last images haunt my dreams. When I think of my father, this image of him, of his last act, dominates my memories. I want to remember the times he danced with delight, the broad smile on his face after a practical joke, or the song he used to sing to me as a child. That song is playing hide and seek with me in this ruinous recollection.

Sometimes, in dreams, I see my dad quietly weeping with my mother at my grandparents' grave. When I was a child on holiday in Sri Lanka, I empathetically cried with them. I wondered why my father and mother were so sad when mourning their parents, but seeing their grief overcame me. I didn't understand their pain at the time, but I knew I would one day. I shared their sadness, hoping to absorb it and free them of their pain. It broke my heart to see my parents cry because they were such resolute people. They made me realize that compassion and kindness were a type of superpower.

As I weep in the front seat of the ambulance, I understand the loss of a parent and remember how terrible a lesson it was to learn. I know this horrific reminiscence is about to end, and I pivot my mind to the music. The ambulance radio plays the same song I've heard throughout this replayed experience. I know it is a clue regarding my past and a link to my father. Is it a Beatles song?

I look at Branko again to my left. He sheds tears and snuggles closely into my body. He is sharing the pain of my father's death so soon after the loss of our Aliba. What a loss for this poor little fellow.

Aliba is another casualty in the nightmare of life. She and my father are gone. The man who gave me my surname is no more. My father's name is Shelton Perera. This elucidation runs through me like an electric shock and causes my eyes to close.

●●●

When my eyes reopened, they were confronted by the body of a blood-covered mother monkey. My mother Aliba was dead. Even monkey CPR won't change that fact.

15
CREMATION

A soft rubbing on the back of my hand brought me back to the harsh reality of my surroundings. As focus cleared my vision, despair filled my heart.

Nishpunk's large sobbing face loomed above me. Perhaps he thought me dead alongside my mother. He smiled as I sat up, resurrected from the jungle floor. He had sharp splinters of wood protruding from his trunk and large bloody welts on his face and body. It seemed whatever attacked Aliba had to go through Nishpunk first.

The cuts and abrasions on his face indicated that stones had been propelled at him. The damage to Aliba's body was similar, akin to an execution by stoning. Monkeys were not so different from human beings. In Sharia law, women are executed in front of a gathered crowd if they have committed the offense of forbidden love. Aliba's only crime was trying to protect her son; her love for a strange monkey had ended her life.

In the same way I failed my father, I have failed my mother in the jungle. Not only have I let Aliba down, but I have also betrayed Branko. Rather than worrying about my human family, I have been living in a dream world, halfway between monkey and boy. The consequence of trying to be both has left me doing neither satisfactorily. I was endangering my family in the jungle and the sentence was death. I felt like I had lost both a mother and a father in one day.

However, I was not an orphan because my human mother was in England! I will truly have let Aliba down if I do not return to my human family.

I rubbed Nishpunk's trunk and removed the splinters that were dug into his skin. I then attempted to lift Aliba's body but was too weak to raise her limp carcass from her sullied resting place.

Nishpunk saw my attempt and moved toward her body. He approached slowly and cradled her head with the tip of his trunk. He then gently eased beneath her body, and she rose from the ground, supported by his strength.

I walked before my elephant brother, and in tandem we formed an unusual but dignified burial procession. As we staggered along toward the river, Branko wailed in agony at the loss.

His cries reverberated throughout our surroundings. The jungle had become silent in tribute to our mourning, yet something more sinister was afoot. Quiet in the jungle was more likely to mean danger than safety. The monkeys who attacked Nishpunk and Aliba were likely to strike again.

The jungle was no longer safe for either of us.

Upon seeing a small enclave of trees beside the river, I instructed Nishpunk to set Aliba down and then skipped around some nearby rocks. We covered her fragile body with stones, leaves, and twigs.

Before I covered her face, I kissed her forehead. "I am so sorry, mother. This will not be your final resting place, but I do not have the materials to send you on your journey. I will return to give you a fitting funeral appropriate for a Buddhist."

I needed to get the necessary items from Gabriel's cabin and return here immediately. The impact of the day's events had not tired me. My only reservation about returning to the logging camp was Nishpunk's safety whilst I was away. I would take him with me to the site, but I couldn't fathom how to get him over the river. I attempted to reassure the brute by stroking him gently, but he charged into the jungle as I ran to the bridge. I imagine he thought I was abandoning him again and wasn't prepared to be left alone and vulnerable. The journey back to the cabin was swift, and my mind drifted into the past.

●●●

Suddenly, I am sitting in the back of a car surrounded by my family, with one notable exception. My father is not present because we are traveling to his cremation, and his body is in the funeral hearse ahead of us.

The mood is unusually jovial given the sorrowful circumstances. Everyone is trying to lift each other's spirits with stories about my father. Jokes, anecdotes, and heart-warming tales fill the conversation throughout the thirty-minute journey. The story of how my father asked my mother to marry him seven times is told for the thousandth time. The way his chest filled with pride when watching his beloved Sri Lanka in cricket. His (rather annoying) celebratory dancing jig when Manchester United scored a goal.

The reality of the situation hits us like a sledgehammer as we pull up to the crematorium. We have been telling stories about a man no longer alive. In a short while, his body will be turned to ash; his soul has probably already gone to another place. I wonder if he will remember this life with my family once he has moved on to his next. I like to think he would be reincarnated as a lion cub in Africa, the king of the jungle, and the top of the food chain. This thought used to comfort me as I wept before falling asleep in the weeks after his death.

●●●

My sad memory faded, and I was in Gabriel's cabin retrieving the lighter before heading back to Aliba's body. I hoped Nishpunk would return to the burial site. I did not want to embark upon a cremation alone. I gathered some flammable-looking pieces of wood. As I struggled to carry the weight, Nishpunk emerged from behind a copse of trees. He didn't venture too far away, probably due to fear and in the hope I would return. I was thrilled to see him—he was one of my few friends in this jungle, and I was soothed by his company during this somber moment.

He helped me to dig Aliba out of her cocoon and place her on some tinder wood. I created a tent with the remaining wood placed over her body. Nishpunk and I then covered the flammable structure with as many dry sticks and leaves as we could find. I wanted her body to be covered entirely in kindling.

When I could no longer see her form, I tried to convince myself this was an anonymous heap of jungle detritus; however, contained in this pile of wood and leaves was the body of my mother.

I lit the smaller pieces of touchwood and sat back with Nishpunk. The creation of fire is one of the most primitive acts a boy or monkey can experience. As I watched the smoke hovering over lumps of logs, I considered my next move.

Aliba was dead, her soul already drifting through space and time, searching for her next life experience. Without her presence in the jungle, I had no reason to remain.

My family's name was *Perera*. I now had a way of finding them.

16
DYING

Nishpunk and I watched the smoke rising from the cremation heap. The acrid plumes began to billow, and the taste of the burning corpse of my mother made me nauseous. It was our duty to stay by the fire until it died out. Then Aliba will be departed, and my time in the jungle will come to an end.

Nishpunk and I drifted into a sorrowful slumber. My weary mind felt weighed down by grief, and I rested my head on the elephant's trunk and elapsed into a trance-like sleep. A reddish-black color covered my vision as my eyelids fluttered. Sleep was necessary, and I was calmed by Nishpunk's familiar rubbing of my hand as I fell into a dream.

●●●

The smell of charred monkey flesh and hair unsettled my subconscious. Initially, I wake up in my dream and am in the family nest.

Aliba is next to me. She walks away from the nest and picks up a shiny metallic object. She flicks open the top of the object and turns to face me. Her eyes are red with flames, and she bares her teeth in anger. She points in an accusatory manner and hisses with venom. Finally, she puts the lighter's flame to her fur and begins screaming like a banshee as the fire engulfs her body.

Her wailing raises the hairs on my neck and penetrates to the core of my bones. Confronted by the fiery suicide of my mother, I close my eyes in terror.

When I open my eyes again, I am in another unfamiliar place but with a familiar smell. The smell of disinfectant mixed with blood and vomit. The walls of the room are a minty, medicinal green. It is a private room, and the human body I inhabit is attached to various wires, leading to monitors and tubes feeding in blood and other life-sustaining fluids.

Whose body is this? I don't remember ever spending time being treated in a hospital in my human life. My most significant memories of being in a hospital are those from when I visited my father.

I try to move my hands first and then my feet, but my body is paralyzed. I attempt to open my mouth but am unable. Why am I here? As I ponder the significance of this memory, a ray of sunshine enters the room. I could not turn my head but peer left to see a shaft of sunlight that had landed on my bed. It almost looks like an arrow guiding my vision. I follow the direction of the arrow and look right as a second ray of sunshine appears in this dank hospital room. My Turkish girlfriend is sitting beside me. Ashley is holding my left hand! The sight of her cherubic face, soft brown hair falling onto her shoulders, and rosy red lips prompt rejoicing in my mind that is not audible from my mouth. I thank an unknown higher power for this heavenly vision and realize he was directing me with arrows of divine sunshine toward my love. I quiet the confusion in my head and consider the reality of this.

Was I hurt shortly before my death? Is this a memory from immediately after whatever accident occurred? Did she wait by my bedside, hoping I would recover? *I wish I could speak to you and console you, my love.* My mind is trapped in this paralyzed body, and even more frustrating is the fact I am thousands of miles away inside the brain of a monkey.

Ashley's eyes are full of tears, and I sense she is about to speak. She continues to hold my hand and rub it reassuringly. I can feel this but am unable to react to her touch. She croaks out a few words, and I listen intently.

"Baby, I love you so much. I am not sure if you can hear me." She starts weeping, slow and despondent. She makes little exhalations as she whimpers rhythmically. Droplets escape her eyes and run down her nose, falling onto her lap. "If you can hear me, please know I do not blame you for what happened."

Blame me for what? As I consider this question, I feel a sudden sharp pain in my heart. Ashley jumps up from the bed and screams. "Oh my God! Don't leave me! Nurse! *Nurse!*" She hits an alarm button to my side. The pain in my chest is crippling, but I realize my eyes can focus. I look at Ashley, and she stares desperately back at me. The pain in my chest forces me to close my eyes.

●●●

I felt Ashley's touch on my hand, but when I opened my eyes, I found Nishpunk's trunk rubbing the same spot where my girlfriend's hand had been only a moment ago.

The impact of this memory left me sitting awestruck. In the last twenty-four hours, I had found the body of my dead primate mother and cremated her. I had relived the nightmare of my father dying. Before I considered if it could get any worse, I realized I may have also relived the moment *I* died! Not only that I had perished, but the final acts of my life may had involved me doing something horrendous to the person I love the most, Ashley.

Nishpunk grabbed my hand, and I realized he was waking me from my sleep for a reason. We were surrounded by primates, and lying ahead of me was the strangest looking pig I had ever seen. I can only describe this monstrosity as the *Monkeyfacedpig.*

17
REVENGE

The monkeyfacedpig walked up to me standing upright. It had the body of a pig, with trotters, a rotund tummy covered in pink skin dotted with black spots. However, the thing's face was that of a deformed monkey. It had two bulgy eyes, close together, somewhat similar to a chimp but much uglier. Black skin covered the face, and its mouth and chin were covered with grey fur. Its face was almost hypnotic due to how hideous it was to behold.

The throng of primates surrounding me was so silent you could hear a pin drop. The monkeyfacedpig stopped before me and began singing:

A year of sweat, year of tears, year of blood, year of fear.
How do you measure the length of a year?
In seconds, minutes, days, weeks, and months?
The time it takes to revolve around the sun?
Five hundred twenty-five thousand and six hundred minutes.
How do you measure the length of a year?
A year of sweat, year of tears, year of blood, year of fear.

He promptly stopped singing and then asked me a question. "How do you measure the length of a year, Branko? How do you measure the loss of a life?"

The three Hs were promptly marched out by two woolly spider monkeys and pushed down on their knees before me. None of the trio looked into my eyes. As they mournfully settled with their heads down on their chests, the arm of every primate rose into the air. Each hand contained a stone.

The monkeyfacedpig addressed me again. "I know what these three have taken from you. Now, you must decide their fate. The loss of your mother was not the wish of the Monkeyfacedpigking! Now you have a choice Branko. Should they live, or should they perish after they took the mother you cherished?"

Regardless of the bizarre nature of my surroundings or the disgusting, regal atrocity dictating these events, I knew I had to make a decision. Anger boiled within me, but then my father's voice echoed in my mind. *They say revenge is a dish best-served cold, but I think it is better never served at all.* My decision was made, and I announced, "In the words of the Lord Buddha, we must replace hate and revenge with kindness, tolerance, and forgiveness."

I can speak!

The Monkeyfacedpigking burst into laughter. "Of course you can speak, but only in this place. I can hear your words and see your thoughts. You have made the correct decision, and the three Hs will be freed—but only after they receive the banana punishment of forgiveness."

I responded so fast it was as if my mouth hadn't even opened, "I would prefer they received no punishment whatsoever."

The Monkeyfacedpigking stood unmoved, "That is not your decision to make, my insolent half-monkey, half-human."

How can this creature know so much about me? Can this awful beast really read my thoughts?

"Yes, I can. And I would much prefer not to be called a monstrosity, hideous, or a beast. After all, I am just an unusual creation of nature, just like you. Nothing more, nothing less."

I had to try and switch off my brain for the moment.

"Okay, Branko. If you are going silent, I will do the thinking, as you are in much need of direction. Would you like to hear a poem?" This wasn't a question, as I could see the monkeypig readying himself to proclaim a poetic verse. He stood up tall on the toes of his rear trotters, raised his front two trotters to silence the crowd, and began reciting words in a shrill singing voice that was quite shocking to my ears:

THE BOY IN THE MONKEY

Ode to the orangutan
Oh, dearest uncle?
You rang, you rang.
Oh, dearest uncle?
You rang, you rang.
You giggle as we meet.
So bitter and yet so sweet.
When you are happy,
how doth the bananas flow!
But if du bist angry…
oranjes will boom
and donkeys will weep.
When will the trumpets sound
and signal your defeat?
Dear old friend Uncle Orangutan.

"What did you think? What did you think?"

Why was this Monkeypigthing reading me poetry? I offered my honest appraisal of the poem. The crowd waited silently, and I knew I should withhold any unnecessarily negative feedback. "It was rather simple, but I liked it. I like the comparison between humans and monkeys. After all, we are pretty much the same."

All the primates began to laugh. It seemed I was performing a riotous comedy performance without actually trying to.

"Branko, do you know who wrote that poem?" exclaimed the monstrous creature.

"No. Was it you, Monkeyfacepigking?" I replied honestly, hoping that the suggestion might be considered a compliment.

The leader of the throng sneered as he spoke, "Oh no, I am no poet. I am only a king. I have many gifts but not this remarkable skill. Would you like to hear another one?"

I got the feeling this was also not a question.

"You are correct; I was not asking your permission," and the pigking sang the following words in the piercing, high pitch that had become etched on my brain:

Monkey circus where we laugh
ha-ha-ha-ha-ha-ha-ha-ha-ha-ha-ha-ha-ha!
Monkey do monkey say
all of us end in heaven
      Dig-a-dig ding-dang ding-dang dong
      Dig-a-dig ding-dang ding-dang dong
Bobo monkey makes us laugh
as he dances like a demon,
hear the crack of the whip
as we punish his poor brethren!
      Dig-a-dig ding-dang ding-dang dong
      Dig-a-dig ding-dang ding-dang dong
Monkey say monkey do
all of us end in heaven.
Monkeys on trapeze!
Watch his brother fly
      Dig-a-dig ding-dang ding-dang dong
Gibbons adorned with ribbons
cartwheeling with glee!
Orang-U-clowns make children go weeee!
Squirrel monkeys dancing funky
      Dig-a-dig ding-dang ding-dang dong
      Lemurs going mental!
Bush babies, marmosets, colobus in dresses.
Bearded ladies, altered nature
when will this madness end?
      Dig-a-dig ding-dang ding-dang dong
Suddenly not all laughing,
grave change of mood.
Nature altered, abuse to monkey,
all will end in rage.
      Dig-a-dig ding-dang ding-dang dong
Laughter turns to fear
monkeys start to leer!
Staring into youthful tears
silence to the vengeful jeers.
      Dig-a-dig ding-dang ding-dang dong
      Never again shall the whip crack
on another monkey's hairy back.
Tonight, the monkeys shall be free
but first, every child shall bleed!"

Before I had a meaningful chance to consider the trauma of what I had heard and witnessed, the king addressed me inquisitively.

"What do you think it means?" asked the Monkeyfacedpigking.

"The dig-a-dig ding-dang ding-dang dongs were a bit much, to be honest. However, it seemed to be about the coming together of monkeys and humanity, as well as crimes against nature. I liked it, but thought it a bit juvenile!" Again, I seemed to state something quite hilarious. Every monkey in the house was crying tears of joy.

"Oh, Branko, this is why we love you so much. Simple and juvenile! Hahaha. Well, the throng will tell you who wrote those poems. Tell the monkeyman!" On the king's command, the ensemble screamed and pointed at me.

"YOU DID! YOU DID! YOU DID!" They screamed it over and over again.

I yelled back at the mob, "Stop! What do you mean I wrote those poems?"

The king raised a trotter, and the crowd was silenced, "Well, Branko, as a boy, you showed us monkeys a lot of compassion. You used to write a lot of poems, some of which were about us. Big Dave the red howler loves hanging out around the computers near the logging camp. Well, through the power of the internet, he managed to come by your majestic poetry. We like it very much. Your poems made us happy."

Furious and perplexed, I retorted, "Is that why I am here, because of some stupid monkey poems?"

The monkey-mob did not appreciate that phrase. I regretted it immediately, partly because of the hissing and spitting directed at me but also because I suddenly remembered a love for my poetry.

Outrage was evident in the king's voice. "Stupid monkey poems! Those verses are the only reason you are still in this world. We could have left you stuck between life and death and you would never have had a chance of getting back to your family. You showed us a lot of affection. That is why Branko saved you, but we can no longer tolerate your presence. You are no longer welcome in the Monkeyfacedpig's kingdom. Leave now, or you will endure a banana punishment followed by a stoning!"

"Look, I apologize for my actions. They were hasty. Please let me ask a few more questions. Why am I here? How do I get home? What is the name of the person who wrote those poems?"

"Silence!" The crowd fell silent, and so did I.

"Your audience with the king is at an end. As your poems have brought me joy, I will offer you one more piece of advice." He paused and waved his hand toward the three Hs. They were approached by a gang of black bearded saki, who monkeyhandled them and wedged their heads between the branches of three trees. To a chorus of snarling, hissing, chattering, and wailing (from the three Hs), the sakis forced a large, unripe banana into each of their murderous monkey bottoms. Remorse streamed from the eyes of my mother's killers.

Although I did not believe in revenge, I gained a certain amount of joy from witnessing this act that the Lord Buddha would have been disappointed to see. Three monkeys making three bananas disappear without eating them, now *that* is a magic trick!

The king looked back at me and stared for a long time. "You blame yourself for actions beyond your control. That is how you ended up here. My final advice is to inform you that it is not your fault."

With that announcement, the primates marched away from a lonely monkey. It just occurred to me that Nishpunk had abandoned me. He was probably scared and decided to flee.

"Your friend the elephant has returned to his family. He has had enough of charging around with a delinquent monkey. I suggest you go back to your family also. Oh—and please don't return to my jungle again."

I knew my audience with the Monkeyfacedpigking was over as he let out an exceptional fart as he turned and walked away. The noise as the gas escaped from his sphincter was unexpectedly high-pitched, and the sound could be described as a squeaker. However, the smell—which was truly striking—resonated with a pungent mixture of rotten herring and Limburger cheese. The aroma was so dense it felt like you could take a bite out of the surrounding air. However, if you did, you'd probably drop down dead.

18
EXPRESSION OF LOVE

I left Aliba's cremation site and was surrounded by an old foe, encircled by an enemy I could not escape. That nemesis penetrated my strongest defenses, crippled my mental well-being, and paralyzed me physically. I was alone, and the reality of being confronted by my greatest fear was terrifying.

As a human, on family trips to the shops, my older brothers took responsibility for looking after me. They used to pretend to lose me in amongst the crowd. I vividly remembered that fear as I realized I might have been forgotten and might be alone. In my past life, I was the sort of person who loved being surrounded by friends and family, by the people I love. Time alone was just an opportunity to think and reflect on the reality of life and self-induced pain.

The loss of my father made these periods alone traumatic. They left me to consider if I had made the right choices in the moments leading to his death. Could I have saved him? Perhaps if I had listened intently in my first aid classes at school? I will always wonder if I could have saved his life and will always blame myself for his death.

Then I wondered if I was a good son. My life changed when he died. That event spurred me on to become the person I became. I hoped he was proud of the misdirected young man I was whilst he was alive. He never saw me become something. He died not knowing that I cherished every moment with him and worshipped the wisdom he offered. Losing people can crush your spirit.

Now, time alone allowed my mind to wander to recent consequences. Had my actions led to the death of Aliba? As I walked the jungle floor, guilt overwhelmed my fragile mind. My actions seemed to lead to the deaths of those closest to me. What good could possibly occur if I burst back into my girlfriend's and family's lives? This felt like the lowest moment of my second life, but a recollection from my first life lifted my spirits.

My mother and I traveled to Vienna after my dad died. We spent four days together, seeing the sights before she returned to London, and I continued on a European tour. I remembered preparing to say goodbye when she was about to leave on a bus to the airport. She came to me and put her arms around my waist. She is only five feet tall, so I engulfed her when I hugged her small frame. However, the strength of the hug she gave me squeezed all the air from my body. The memory of that hug was enough to make me smile. Somehow, even though there had been such a dramatic shift in time, space, and dimension, I could still feel the comfort of that embrace, and it left me breathless.

I was going to return to that hug to my mother, Anne. It was the most beautiful expression of love I could imagine, making me feel human again.

19
REMEMBERING THE ANIMAL

I entered the infirmary quietly, not wishing to wake one of my few remaining comrades, and sat beside Gabriel. He looked very poorly as he lay in his bed. I wondered how long it would be until I notched another casualty on my stained conscience. I was the monkey harbinger of doom. Without Gabriel and Christa, I had no way back to my family. They could be my last chance, but could I take the burden of another death? At this thought, Gabriel awoke and leaned over to hug me. He strained and retreated back into his bed. Seeing his weakened state, I jumped onto the mattress and nestled under his arm.

"Why such a sad face, little one?" he asked. "I have never seen a monkey look so depressed. To be fair, I haven't had a monkey for a friend before!"

Not wanting to lower Gabriel's morale, I chose to keep the loss of Aliba from him. Regarding the Monkeyfacedpigking, I decided to keep this information to myself as well. It was strange enough being a boy in a monkey, but if I tried to explain random hallucinations, primate dances, death challenges, psychotic mind reading, crossbred monkeypig poets, people might think I've lost my mind.

The worrying thing was that it might be the most rational explanation. The realm I was in did not seem to have an identifiable animal or human perspective. In fact, I seemed lost in limbo between reality and the surreal, but maybe the world of animals was far more magical than humans gave it credit for?

At that moment, Christa opened the infirmary door and, seeing me yelped with delight, ran over to me and scooped me into her embrace. A hug worthy of a mother and precisely the sort of healing contact my body craved. Her warmth and affection were like a sunny Sunday afternoon you never wanted to end.

She put me down on the bed and asked me the million-dollar question, "Do you know your family name?"

I nodded.

Gabriel reached to his side and grabbed a pen and paper pad. He handed me the tools and said enthusiastically, "Give me all you've got. We can use that info to find a link to your family."

I wrote the name of my oldest brother, Amal Perera, then my middle brother, Sidath, my father, Shelton, and finally my mother, Anne. I didn't know where this would lead, but it would start with an email to my brother that would explain that his dead brother was now sharing the body of a baby monkey. In terms of emails, this was surely so bizarre that my brother would know it couldn't be a hoax.

As if reading my mind, as I considered my brother's probable reaction, Christa asked another question: "What on earth are you going to say to them? Either way, we are all going to sound like complete lunatics!" Christa was blunt in nature, and although this point was tactless, it was accurate. I needed to develop a thicker skin, as being precious wasn't going to get me home.

How should I explain this situation? Gabriel responded to Christa's insensitive comment. "We may be lunatics, but Branko will be able to win them over with information only a family member would know."

That's it! I sat and thought of my relationship with my brother Amal. I knew his wife's name was Shama and his daughter's was Ava, but any internet search could gain that information. I needed things personal to him and me. Why wouldn't my memory-deficient brain offer me some assistance? Though the last thing I needed was another reminder of my father's passing, my mind was suddenly illuminated by a crystal-clear memory. *I used to call Amal my second dad!*

Slowly, the experiences we shared as brothers became clearer in my mind. I used to call Amal my second dad because he was ten years older than me and was always very responsible. He tried to teach me how to box when I was ten years old, but one of my jabs penetrated his defenses, and I left him with a bloody nose. His friends used to call him *Animal* as a nickname. He was an excellent cricketer and taught me to play in our back garden. I was the last person in the house before he left for his wedding vows at the registry office.

●●●

It is half past eight in the morning, and I have just returned from holiday with my schoolmates in Portugal. I am sleep-deprived and have been out far too often drinking, but Amal just told me he was very nervous, so I sat with him.

He grabs a bottle of whiskey from the liquor cupboard and pours us both a measure of scotch. The last thing I need is a scotch at eight-thirty in the morning, but I know he wants a drink to settle his nerves. So down the hatch it goes.

It tastes awful. To make things worse, the last time I tasted whiskey was seven years ago, which was the first time I had ever tasted alcohol.

The first double scotch for breakfast isn't the end of my torture. Amal's nerves are not resolved with one double measure of whiskey, so he pours another two glasses. I can feel the burning sensation as the fiery liquid flows down my throat and into my belly.

We leave for his wedding, slightly inebriated, at barely nine in the morning. I can't imagine wives look kindly upon the fact that their husbands need a little Dutch courage before committing to a lifetime of 'blissful' matrimony, but this is the way we live our lives, sharing our experiences as one. Hopefully, she won't find out.

Now, after Amal's wedding, as the bride and groom prepare to leave the hall, Amal, Sidath, and I come together for one final embrace. We are no longer brothers who will reside under the same roof, and that realization brings a measure of sadness.

No more arguing over football matches that led to brawls in the living room. My mum would never again line us up in a row and feed us in a set order, largest to smallest, from hand to mouth, from one plate of food (amazingly, we were fed this way from toddlers until Amal left the house at twenty-nine years old). So, we hug and cry in the hall on the happiest day of my oldest brother's life.

Family and friends look on, but only those who have truly loved empathize with our loss. Those jealous of our intimacy mock our sorrow.

●●●

I felt as if that was the requisite detail to convince my brother that the email was not a hoax and this monkey was for real.

20
KARMIC MONKEY

Gabriel and I sat by his computer. He had the exuberant look of a child just before opening a Christmas present, such was his lofty expectations of my potential.

I hit the enter key and the internet searched for *Amal Perera*. It was a wonder of the modern age that a boymonkey could easily find his human brother.

The first result was a social network webpage listing Amal Perera's name. To my amazement, when I clicked on the result, a picture of my second dad appeared in front of my face. I hit the link to his webpage and immediately saw pictures of his baby daughter, Ava. She seemed so much bigger than I remembered. She was more a small person as opposed to a baby.

How long have my mind and soul been away? Three months, six months, perhaps even more? A year? How ridiculous will it seem when I contact them? Their son, their brother, their relative who had been dead for a year and now masquerading as a monkey in the jungle! Was this fate playing a cruel trick on me? I know I appreciated monkeys in my previous life, but ending up as one was crazy karma.

Last night, I struggled to sleep. Whilst inhabiting the space outside real life that resided in the dream world, I was visited by a familiar memory. I was in child form and attending a Buddhist sermon at my local temple. I looked to my right and saw my dad beside me. He listened intently while sitting in an uncomfortable half-lotus, almost cross-legged position. I was eager to get outside and enjoy a bit of sunshine and play with some of the other children. However, because my dad was listening to the sermon, I decided to follow his lead and see if this bald-headed fellow in orange robes spoke any sense.

In a shrill, unnaturally high-pitched Sri Lankan accent that strangely reminded me of the monkeyfacepig, the priest began, "Before we are born in this world, while still in the realms of spirit and along with our higher guides, we decide the lessons we shall pursue on earth. Spirit helps us pursue these lessons by creating the conditions necessary to receive our chosen experience. What is the experience you would like to pursue? How will your next life offer you the conditions to achieve your destiny?

"Karma is not about punishment. In spirit, there is no absolute right or wrong. It is about experience and fulfillment of purpose. The idea that we are punished for sins is a man-made form of social control. You will not inhabit the form of a beetle or a diseased man as a punishment. This will be your fulfillment of purpose. You will move one step further to enlightenment if you conduct yourself appropriately."

This sermon had been lost on me as a child. However, for obvious reasons, it seemed to impart more resonance regarding my current circumstances. As I tucked my feet under my thighs and adopted a perfect lotus position, I noticed my brothers in front of me sniggering and not paying any attention to the sermon. Funnily enough, I never listened to the sermons because they were in Singhalese, and I don't speak my parents' mother-tongue.

"The first step in dealing with existing karma is awareness and acknowledgment. Are there any themes that seem to recur throughout your life? Nothing happens by chance. Recurrent themes suggest the hand of karma. These recurrent themes tell you they provide conditions for some necessary life experience."

What themes have I experienced in my life as Branko? Loss seems to be a recurring theme in my life. And being able to deal with it. The consequences of my actions keep confronting me. Why did my actions lead to other people getting hurt? Every step I took led to someone dying.

"The second aspect of karma is that it is always created. Every act of will, every thought, is a karmic act. By acting in accordance with our spiritual purpose in particular—and spiritual principles in general—we create good karma for tomorrow. But good karma doesn't mean *material success*; it is concerned with *spiritual progress*."

So, my journey was a karmic act. Perhaps I had to rectify an ill caused in my previous life, and karma had allowed me to do this in my new form. I have been given a second shot at life, perhaps at redemption, and I have returned in the form I so revered. *What lessons must I learn on the road to spiritual enlightenment?*

As I reminisced over this thought, Gabriel rubbed my back and woke me from my daydream slumber. I had been staring at the screen for a while. The mouse was highlighting an email address on Amal's social media page. Gabriel copied the address and pasted it into an email.

"Now is your chance to convince him you are his brother. Write him something magnificent."

21
WOULD YOU REPLY TO THIS EMAIL?

It took me the best part of two days to structure the bizarre content of this email. I struggled to put words together and didn't know how to approach the subject matter. In the end, I decided to offer some specific information and yet refrain from informing my brother I had taken the form of an ape child. As you can imagine, trying to win someone over via email and telling them you are a monkey did not necessarily go hand in hand.

The question I kept repeating to myself was, *would I respond to such an email?* The unfortunate answer was quite obviously, *no*. It read like a ponzi-scheme email written by someone on hallucinogenic drugs.

Dear Amal,

Whatever you do, please read this email to the end, as this message relates to a huge windfall that you are entitled to! This is not a hoax. I am a very close family friend of yours. Indeed, you could even call me a long-lost relative. Currently, I am residing in Brazil and, due to visa-related reasons, cannot return to England. We have met, but it was a long time ago under very different circumstances. Please persevere with this elaborate email. There is a reason behind this unusual message.

I want to state a few truths. These are intimate facts about your family, childhood, and life. I hope they will confirm I am indeed your relative. The explanation for me knowing this information is that I knew your father before he died. I promise this letter will ultimately make sense.

Your name is Amal Perera. You are the oldest son of Shelton and Anne Perera. You are married to Shama and have a daughter named Ava. I know anyone can find that information with a quick internet search, but please read on.

You have a scar below your right eye on your cheek. You tell people you got it playing cricket. The truth, though, is that you got drunk when you were sixteen and fell over in the bathroom, hitting your head on the toilet bowl and knocking yourself out. You were found with your pants down by your mother.

Your favorite malt whiskey is Macallan. I know this because you drank it on the morning of your wedding.

Your youngest brother bought you a terrible painting as a present for your wedding. It was of three dogs playing poker. Shama hates it, and it is currently hanging in your downstairs toilet.

Your daughter Ava is named after your grandmother, a woman you never had the opportunity to meet. She was an amazing woman who overcame prejudice to become a doctor in 1950s Sri Lanka. However, she committed suicide when she found out her husband was having an affair.

You wear your father's wedding ring on your left hand next to your own wedding ring. You have worn this since the day he died, May 14th, 1997.

You and your brothers used to play cricket in the back garden, which you renamed the Cauldron. Your brothers inevitably fought when they played, and you usually acted as the mediator. A match in the Cauldron typically ended with your youngest brother crying.

When teaching your youngest brother to box, he struck your nose and fractured it. He was ten years old. He used to call you his second dad as a child because you always looked out for him.

I know it will be extremely difficult for you to believe I am your relative, but ask yourself how I could have known the information above if I wasn't. I am currently stuck in Brazil but would like to be in regular contact with you. I am experiencing difficulties with immigration in terms of returning to the UK. However, my aim is to return to London and meet you and your family.

Apologies for misleading you regarding the potential jackpot at the start of the email. I desperately needed you to read to the end of this communication and hope you will reply to me. I apologise for the lack of detail. At this point, I simply want to be in contact with you and reacquaint myself with our family. I just want to communicate with you and pray you will receive this email and feel a desire to reply.

Love from your relative.

22
FORGETTING ME

I waited anxiously for a day, which became a week, and that turned into an eternity. However, as the excitement of the unknown turned into sadness and despair, a new problem emerged.

A few strange events began to worry me. Gabriel had encouraged me to write another email to my brother. Rather than commit it to the screen straight away, I decided to scribe a letter on paper. However, as I attempted to write the words onto the page, I found my hand could not communicate with my brain. As I tried to write letters on the page, the pen became uncomfortable in my hand and all I could manage were illegible scribbles. It was as if I had forgotten how to write. The pen didn't feel right in my grip. It felt like a foreign object, and I had an urge to smash it into pieces.

Unable to communicate this issue to Gabriel, I put down the pen and contemplated the degradation of my mind. Could my time in Branko's company be limited? Was my inability to write a sign I might be starting to forget me? Is that what someone with Alzheimer's experienced? Knowing that your faculties were depreciating and no way to slow down the erosion of your identity?

Later that same evening, I concentrated on imagining my family's faces. I could see them in my mind's eye but could not remember their names. It seemed my Swiss cheese brain would continue to lose memories from my past. The recollections of my family that I treasured slipped like grains of sand through my fingers. For every memory I recalled, it felt like I was losing two more.

The real worry, however, was forgetting a fundamental function like writing. To lose the power of communication would leave me imprisoned in this body forever. What if my family became an irretrievable memory? To lose the anchor of my family would leave my soul in limbo. Perhaps this was the necessary conclusion, as my soul and memories were never supposed to survive into this next existence?

I sat in the canopy overlooking the jungle surrounding the logging camp. For the first time, I was disconsolate. My brother Amal could not save me from this situation, and my memory was rapidly diminishing. My time was limited, so I sat, breathed deeply, calmed my mind, and considered the memories I did retain.

Searching through the emptiness of an amnesia-riddled mind was an extremely exhausting process that required intense concentration and discipline. Before I fell asleep from weariness, I descended from my vantage point and headed towards Gabriel's cabin.

I was extremely drowsy and stumbled through the branches as I headed to the ground. I saw a large puddle ahead of me and took a small jump into it, expecting to spring out of the water. Instead, my feet became stuck in the mud. With each struggle, I slipped deeper into the murk. Within seconds, I was submerged to the neck, and with a few last wiggles, I was up to my nostrils.

One last breath: a last intake of air before an ignominious death and end to my struggle. The ground was retaking the soul that escaped it in my previous life. My nose went under the muddy surface, and I took a final look up to the trees as my head went under.

I panicked and inhaled water, which was probably the worst thing you can do when submerged. As the water permeated my eyes, I blinked uncontrollably in panic and screamed, releasing the last of the air in my defiant lungs. I kept falling while inhaling dirty water and desperately wishing for the torture to cease.

Suddenly, I stopped tumbling and felt the pressure of the mud release my legs. A space might be below me, so I struggled and descended through the grime. If I could drop through to that space below, I'd be able to breathe.

I made it through the sludge and fell into the hollow. I inhaled deeply while simultaneously swallowing residual particles of soil. My main problem had shifted from not enough air to too much of it.

I was plummeting through space, falling into the unknown.

23
BAPI RETURNS

Falling into the unknown should be terrifying, but what was really odd was not knowing when the descent would end. My legs dangled in the emptiness, and as I became more comfortable falling into oblivion, I started making arm windmills and yelling in excitement, "Woooo!" I was reminded that in my human life, I had once skydived out of a plane. Suddenly, I saw my body descending into annihilation with a completely different perspective.

If this was the end, then what a way to go.

I landed with a soft thud, and my body slumped forward. My face was on the floor, and I had assumed an orthodox prayer position that may or may not have been directed toward Mecca. My body should have been broken, but instead, I felt numb. I was unable to lift my head and was confronted with a close-up view of what appeared to be a shaggy carpet in my face. This was not a jungle-variety floor. The fear of the mud burial I was expecting disappeared, but where was this place? Was I hallucinating again?

Then I heard a voice I'd never heard before but immediately recognized.

"Where my monkey? Where my monkey? Where's my monkey? Where's my monkey?"

At the final exclamation, I was lifted from my slumped position and drawn into the most affectionate, bone-crushing hug.

Can it be? Was this a hug from my baby niece? She slobbered on my face and kissed me while giggling with delight. I could not hug her back, but my spirit soared by this impossible embrace.

When Ava was smaller and younger, she would never hug me with the same vigor she embraced her parents. I always wanted to cuddle her like a limpet, to be held tight like she did with them, and I just got my wish.

How had fate conspired for me to be here, reunited with my niece? As this question dominated my thoughts, I was flung to the floor and landed by some glass patio doors. I faced the garden behind my brother's house. I was reminded of my brother's lack of gardening skills. Rotting apples littered the foot-high, unkempt grass and weeds surrounding the garden's periphery where flowers should have been.

My focus suddenly caught my reflection in the glass. A familiar monkey sat before me, but this was not Branko. This was the face of Ava's favorite monkey toy, which I bought her as a present. This man-made monkey had been her companion and best pal since she could crawl. The irony of a boy residing in a real monkey's body occupying an artificial toy monkey was somewhat mind-bending. Was I currently in the fourth dimension? What type of man-made monkey magic voodoo was this, and who determined my destiny? As I considered this conundrum, I heard another familiar voice.

"Ava! Where is monkey?" The reflection of my mother walking into the room was replayed on the glass before me.

"Come on, Ava bubba, go and get your friend, monkey."

My mum walked towards me and gestured to Ava to do the same. Ava looked at her grandmother with a mischievous grin. I could see she was a little terror, but everyone loves a naughty child as they are so much fun.

"Go and get monkey, Ava."

"Nana, that is not monkey."

I was giddy with the thought of what this could potentially mean. What did my niece know, and how could she help me?

"Ava? Then who is it, bubba?" asked my mother.

"Bapa! Bapa! Bapa!"

My mother was visibly shocked by this proclamation. The word *bapa* is Singhalese and means *uncle*. I think my mother knew Ava was not referring to my brother, Sidath. Tears were visible in my mother's eyes, but she quickly wiped them away. "Now, little one, Siddy Bapi is at work, and Mini Bapi is away. How can either of them be here?"

Mini Bapi was my nickname when Ava was very young. It seemed the nickname had stuck even after death. It also seemed my mother was still unable to come to terms with my passing. It was extremely strange to hear yourself mentioned in the past tense, never likely to be in the present tense again.

"No Nana, Mini Bapi is back."

I could feel the lump rising and blocking my throat, and it seemed my mother had the same affliction. It was difficult being confronted with such a vivid reminder of a lost loved one, and Mum was going to be upset by this episode for a long time to come.

She walked to Ava and picked her up for a cuddle. As they hugged, I saw my mother's sadness running down her face.

Ava, with a slightly bemused look, whispered to her grandmother to console her, "Nana, why are you crying? Mini Bapi has to go now. Say bye, Nana. He will be back again soon."

A sudden flash of light forced my eyelids shut. When they opened, I was neck-deep in sludge.

Before me stood the odious, obese man known as Huggins and his wretched dog, Bruno. I seemed to have gotten these nightmares in reverse. I experienced them when awake rather than falling asleep into them.

24
ROASTED FAT

B runo growled and pulled eagerly at the leash, being nearly throttled by the restraint of Huggin's grip.

"Easy, Bruno," he said to his vicious companion. "This little monkey ain't goin' nowhere! You have got yourself in a right pickle, haven't ya? Not quite sure how ya got out of the cage, but looks like you're goin' back in."

Looking up at Huggins's leering swollen face, I considered my options. I was unable to move my body. Only my head was visible in these muddy constraints, and a ferocious, snarling, possibly rabid dog wanted to eat my exposed skull. I hoped Huggins's sweaty palms did not slip on that leash, or Bruno would be eating my monkey brains for lunch. I needed Christa, Gabriel, or Nishpunk to arrive and save me.

As Huggins wiped the sweat from his brow, a small projectile flew at his head and struck him on the side of his temple. As the object hit his stupid face, he pulled a bemused smirk that made him look even dimmer than I could have ever imagined. I expected he adopted the same face whenever he picked his nose and pulled out a treasure before eating it.

I chuckled at the thought as another object struck Bruno on his side. He turned to confront the forest to our right and growled at the anonymous intimidatory peril. The shimmering green of the jungle seemed to split down the middle as if a knife had cut through the trees. The flora bent away from each other as if magnetically opposed.

Bruno's aggressive snarling was replaced by yelps of terror, and he quickly retreated behind Huggins' ample posterior. The plump fellow was too slow of mind and body to consider retreat and simply stood in awe of the unfolding scene before him.

My savior walked out from the jungle and took a small bow. That was quite enough for Bruno, whose predisposition to be loyal to humans was outweighed by his basic instinct for survival. He was free of his master's clammy grasp and sprinted rapidly in the opposite direction of the approaching animal. If I wasn't neck-deep in mud, I would have been following Bruno. It seemed I had an unexpected appointment with the Monkeyfacedpigking.

He approached Huggins on two legs, standing upright, and said, "Well, hello. Aren't you an impressive animal? A pig like me that can walk on two legs! I love eating gluttonous overindulgent humans with a dash of mustard and a heap of sauerkraut."

This was all Huggins could stand, and he began to fall to the floor, his mind capitulating under the duress of unexplainable circumstances. Unfortunately, his fainting, inflated body seemed to be descending right for my head. The Monkeyfacedpigking chortled and shouted, *"Timber!"*

As I saw this colossal cretin falling toward me, I resigned myself to the reality that this was going to hurt. I closed my eyes and waited for an impact that never arrived. When I dared to open my eyes, I saw Huggins's catatonic face hovering over me. He seemed to be floating in the air just above my face. A drop of sweat fell from his flabby chin into my right eyeball. The salt in his sweat stung my eye, and the thought of this repulsive man's coolant inside me made me gag.

Suddenly, the meaty moron ascended into the air and floated toward the jungle. A group of primates were waiting to collect him and the body of Huggins disappeared supported on their shoulders.

The Monkeyfacedpigking walked right up to me in the mud and looked down pitifully as he addressed me. "Would you like to leave your shallow grave?" he said in his Sri Lankan Buddhist monk-like voice.

Any friend would do at this point, so I replied, "Yes, I would appreciate getting out. Can you offer me a trotter?"

"That will not be necessary", the king replied as he glared at the mud around me with eyes that glowed with a red tinge. He seemed to will me out of the mud with the severity of expression and powers of concentration. I emerged like a lollipop from a child's mouth and hovered in the air. The king's telekinesis seemed responsible for Huggins's and my defiance of gravity. This monstrous deformity of nature possessed incomprehensible abilities.

"Why thank you, Branko," he said, having read my thoughts again. "I guess I am monstrously talented!"

Something about Huggins's exit had unsettled me, so I asked, "Where did you take the fat man?"

Unnervingly, while licking his lips, the king replied, "I wasn't joking when I said I liked roasted human crackling with mustard and sauerkraut. The sauerkraut is very difficult to come by, but the primate throng will eat well tonight."

"Monkeyfacedpigking, please do not think me unappreciative," I implored. "But is the death of the pudgy man necessary?"

Apoplectic with an otherworldly rage, the beast's indignation was uncontrollable, "I do think you extremely unappreciative. You will soon realize this is the jungle, and animal law rules this place. Would you rather it be you who we roast this evening? How would you manage to see your family again if you end up as a monkey kebab on my barbeque? What I hate about you most is your indecisiveness. Whether good or bad things happen to you, there's one consistency that you will contemplate, question, and fail to do! You are paralyzed by indecision, and if you continue to be so, you'll never get home!"

Although unethical, I had a straightforward decision to make. Either argue the lost cause that was Huggins's life or pursue whatever help the king may offer me in returning to my family. The choice was easier as each second passed, and my guilt evaporated. "What do you know of my family? How do I get home?"

"I know your girlfriend's name is Ashley. What a pretty name. A bit common, but I bet she's delectable in looks and taste. Is she a bit easy as well? I guess so with a name like Ashley. Wonder what she will think of getting married to a monkey? I think your baby niece also looks delicious, but in a slightly different way. Baby meat is so tender and hard to come by. Maybe I could get you home in return for Ava?"

Without thinking about the consequences of challenging this vile statement, my trigger-happy temper caused me to respond. "I think it best to hold your hideous tongue, Monkeyface, before I rip it out of your malevolent mouth."

The freak's incandescent fury was something to behold. It made me quickly realize how foolish my criticism was, "That wouldn't be a wise move, Branko. Not wise at all. I am here to offer you a token of friendship, and this is how you repay me? We could have been friends and loved each other. A Monkeyfacedpigking *god* and a pathetic human trapped in a monkey's body. I could destroy you at any moment, and you have the nerve to make your ridiculous threats?"

The monkeyfacedpigmonster raised his front trotters and suddenly seemed a gigantic presence looming over me. He then began to silently motion as if conducting an orchestra. Astonishingly, the trees around us moved in reaction, and music emanated from the forest. I immediately recognized the beginning of this classical piece.

It was a song from my past called *Cavalleria Rusticana*. It was my favorite piece as a human—one of the most beautiful things created by humanity. I used to play it when my spirits were low, and it had a calming effect on my soul. His playing this piece of music probably meant my life was at a crossroads. Just hearing it took me back to some of the saddest and happiest moments of my human life. Whenever I heard it, it reminded me of catastrophic loss but also of redemption. That even in the nadir of tragedy, we have the strength to recover.

My furious reaction to the king had left me in a jeopardous position, but I believed he sought to calm the situation. Through some form of intuition, I felt that the king wanted to assist me and guide me in my next steps. Threatening him probably wasn't a good idea, but both our emotions had got out of control. Unfortunately, it seemed I had been reacquainted with another old personality trait: a very quick and ugly temper. The music stopped, and the king's conductor performance came to a standstill. He elegantly fell back to his quadrupedal stance.

Wanting to change my approach at the musical interlude, I decided to try a different approach. My pride as a human never allowed me to take a backward step when compromise was required, but surely this purgatory was a chance for me to learn from my mistakes. "Oh, powerful king," I pleaded. "I apologize for my insolence. Please accept my atonement and know I am but an unworthy and humble servant. I greatly appreciate that piece of music you allowed me to hear."

The king's grotesque features immediately softened, "Pitiful rodent knows the way to the king's heart is through servile flattery of my enormous ego. I, too, love that piece. I played it for you because your time is short. It may be the last meaningful recollection you have of being a human. I will help you one last time, but not because of your sycophantic compliments. Only because within you is something beautiful. It's why you survive to this day and why Branko saved you from hell. Also, because you have offered me the sacrifice of the obese oaf's crackling that we will roast for our consumption. We will smoke his fat and gorge on the result of his greed long into the night. We will smear ourselves with his juices and drink his blood whilst dancing in the moonlight."

Unfortunately for Huggins, I had to make my way home and the king seemed determined to eat him. He will be just another casualty on the list of those who perished because of my actions. Maybe if he didn't eat so many sausages, the Monkeyfacedpigking would not have been so determined to devour him? That may sound like victim blaming, but he really should have laid off the meat. Huggin's morbid obesity really had led to his death, although somewhat sooner than he probably predicted. I'd lost a lot on my journey, but it would have been deceitful to say I would lose much sleep over his fate.

The Monkeyfacedpigking left me with one final comment, and I knew this would be the last time I would have to see his grotesque face: "This is the only advice I will offer you. The dwarf will lead you home. Find him by tonight, or remain in your monkey coffin for the rest of your short life. And I am *not* going to miss you calling me grotesque."

The pigking turned his back to me, and I knew the conversation was over as he emitted a quite immaculate fart as he walked away. The scent secreted was a concoction of stinky tofu, bitter almonds, and rotten onions, which stung my nostrils upon inhalation.

THE BOY IN THE MONKEY

25
THE DWARF

I had to find the dwarf by the evening, but where do you find a dwarf in a jungle?

Panic ensued, and I was not sure if the pigking had affected me with some sort of black magic or if my mind had succumbed to the increasing pressure of my reality. Something had fractured in my fragile cerebrum, and anxiety was overcoming me. I needed to grasp at a thought that could calm my rapidly growing paranoia. The one constant in this deranged, tangled labyrinth was that the madness had always found me, and I didn't have to go searching for it.

Regardless of the highly optimistic perspective that my destiny was inevitable, the pigking also said if I didn't find the dwarf by nightfall, I would be stuck in this monkey shell for the rest of my short life. Might my inescapable denouement result in being stuck in a prison cell within Branko's mind forever?

I ran into the infirmary and frantically searched for Christa and Gabriel. Hysteria quickly transitioned to hopelessness as I sat on the floor with my elbows on my knees and rocked back and forth. I think this despair is what they call a *breakdown*.

When my dad passed away, for the first two months, I would cry myself to sleep. When my mother left our home for work in the morning, I wandered around the empty, lifeless house and called out his name. "Dad... dad... dad..." repeating the word with a broken, sorrowful voice, spluttering an unanswerable request. To this day, I know I wasn't asking a rhetorical question when I called out for my father. I genuinely expected him to answer me and believed I could contact his soul. I could sense his presence all around me. He didn't leave the house after his death. He whispered in our ears as we slept. I pined for him while awake but could never communicate with him in the conscious world.

I saw him in a cloud in Hyde Park on a Sunday afternoon.

He eased my frantic mind whilst I sat in a hammock on a beach in Sri Lanka.

As I slept in the shade of a coconut tree, I felt his reassuring presence each time a wave broke and my hanging bed rocked. I returned to the country of his birth to trace his spirit. It seemed obvious that I had to leave my home in London to find his essence again.

I felt like I had two options after my father's death: find him again or commit suicide. Each time I encountered a reminder of his existence, I found another reason to live. Even posthumously, he walked me away from the brink and kept me alive.

At this moment, alone in the infirmary, I felt the same loneliness as when wandering my family home, calling out for my father. I sat on the floor of the infirmary, alone and defeated. Something caught the corner of my vision as I swayed back and forth. The bright colors of a poster on the wall. A flyer stuck on the notice board advertising some kind of attraction. *What is that horrendous confusion of color?* I sat up, sprang to my feet, and walked toward the flyer.

The words displayed in a garish green font immediately caught my attention, *Shelton's Touring Circus.* Surely, it was more than an unusual coincidence that the proprietor of the circus shared my father's name? This reminded me that my middle name was also Shelton, which my father gave me as a gift.

Below the name of the touring circus was a bright, white face with a round, red nose and curly green hair. A miniature man dressed in clown clothing with a monkey on each shoulder, each juggling fruit. His appearance was bizarre and frightening. I felt drawn to the blackness of the eyes and sharpness of teeth

It was the dwarf who would lead me home.

26
SPRINT

G abriel walked into the room and looked extremely glad to see me. I handed him the poster, and he accepted it willingly. I could see the confusion on his face as he read the pamphlet. I grabbed a pen and a pad and tried to write a message, but I could not form a legible sentence. Panic consumed me again, and I found myself smashing the ground with my fist and screeching in a ferocious fit of frenzied furor. I froze at Gabriel's firm grip on my shoulder. He looked at the flyer and shook his head.

Gabriel spoke nervously, obviously worried at my erratic behavior, "Look Branko, this circus is over three hours' drive away. Even if we leave the jungle, the final performance was last night...I don't even know if they will still be there."

I stared at Gabriel, unable to offer any other means of communication. I hoped my eyes transmitted my desperate need to make this journey.

Gabriel stood solemnly whilst considering his options and then smiled. "Perhaps this touring circus is your route out of the jungle, Branko. It could be your way home. We have to try to make it to them, but I won't be able to drive such a long way. We will need a car and a driver. Unfortunately, I have neither, but I know a lady who might."

I jumped on Gabriel's shoulder, and we left the infirmary. We needed to find Christa and a vehicle. Gabriel stepped into the sunshine and aimed at a large wooden cabin across the courtyard. The camp was empty, and it occurred to me that I had no idea what time of the day it was. Why was the camp so quiet? Where were all the workers? Gabriel opened door after door and shouted for Christa, but she didn't emerge. The same dread that consumed me in the infirmary began to surface again. How much time did I have to make it to the circus? What if the circus had left? Does this signal the end of any chance I have to return home?

Just then, Christa emerged from a cabin dressed in only a towel. "What are you shouting about, Gabriel? It is six o'clock in the morning on a Sunday—the day of rest! What happened? Branko is back!" With an exclamation, she screamed, raised her hands, and sprinted toward me. Christa's towel was not securely fastened, and it fell to the floor as she approached.

She continued to run toward Gabriel and me and grabbed onto us both with delight. Being a monkey, I was naked most of the time, and seeing Christa in this natural state didn't seem unusual. My calm attitude in response to Christa's lack of clothing was obviously not shared by Gabriel, whose face went a deep shade of crimson.

Gabriel tried to utter a few words, but his voice had been erased by the shock of the situation. He gasped for breath, and Christa relaxed her grip in response to his sudden lack of oxygen. Her eyes opened wide in worry, and she eased Gabriel onto the floor. Poor Gabriel's heart has taken enough of a battering over the past couple of weeks, but seeing Christa's naked body might be the straw that caused the camel to have a cardiac arrest!

Christa questioned Gabriel, "What is it, Gabby? Are you having an attack? Oh dear, I am sorry I grabbed you so hard. I was just so excited to see Branko!"

Gabriel began to deeply inhale and take in some much-needed air. He focussed his stare on Christa's eyes to avoid the parts of her anatomy that might cause him to expire. "Just needed a deep breath. Another episode… but feeling better… now."

I hopped off Gabriel's shoulder and grabbed Christa's towel. I offered it to her as she sat by Gabriel.

"Why thank you, Branko. It seems I stripped down to my birthday suit in the excitement!" Christa took the towel and wrapped it around her exposed torso. Gabriel then appeared to recover his faculties.

"Christa, we need to get Branko to the outskirts of the city. It could… be his last chance to get home. We need a car… a car and you to drive us there. There is no time to lose."

Christa looked worried at this request. "But Gabriel, my car is in the shop, and everyone else is away from the camp over the weekend. Apart from—" She jumped from her sitting position and raced around the corner, then shrieked, "It's here! It's here! Huggins's motorbike is parked here, and his keys are in the ignition!"

Gabriel got up, and we walked toward the bike, a gleaming vintage Harley Davidson motorbike with the word *SPRINT* emblazoned on it, black with a red stripe along the chassis. Beside the chopper stood a sidecar with more than enough space for an old man and a monkey. Huggins may have been an oaf, but his choice of motorbike was exemplary.

Gabriel shouted out loud as if to vindicate the theft: *"Well, we are going to have to borrow the bike!* I know it's your pride and joy, but you don't mind, do you Huggins?"* He might have been hoping that Huggins wouldn't hear, but I knew he wouldn't. He had bigger issues to worry about, like his impending roasting by crazed carnivorous primates.

Then, with unusual conviction in his voice, Gabriel forcefully instructed, "Christa, get some clothes on. We have no time to lose! Can you drive one of these things?"

Christa replied with great confidence, "Oh yes. You never forget how to ride a bike."

Surprised, Gabriel replied, "So you have ridden a motorcycle before?"

Christa disappeared into her cabin without answering his question. She ran back out within seconds wearing a pair of jeans, a half-buttoned lumberjack shirt, and flip-flops on her feet.

On her return, she asked, "Sorry, Gabriel. What was that?"

With a worried look on his face, Gabriel asked again, "Have you ridden one of these before?" Christa said nothing, and Gabriel repeated the question impatiently as he climbed into the sidecar. I got in next to him and waited for her answer.

As Christa confidently mounted the bike and strapped on Huggin's helmet, she explained, "As a child, I was surrounded by petrolheads. My father and three brothers were all car and bike crazy. I loved bikes and used to ride them all the time. But my oldest brother was killed in a motorcycle crash when I was fourteen. My mother made all her remaining children promise never to ride a bike again. I have not sat on a motorbike in twenty-five years."

I saw Gabriel motion to offer his condolences, but we were already shooting through the logging camp and on our way to the city before he could. I sat between his legs, peering over the top of the sidecar. Gabriel's fingers gripped the metal sidecar so hard he nearly dented it. Christa may not have ridden in twenty-five years, but you never forget how to ride a bike, and she remembered how to ride fast.

27
OMINOUS GRAFFITI

We sprinted through the winding roads of the jungle at breakneck speed. The road was not much wider than the width of the bike and sidecar, and the road consisted of loose gravel! Christa seemed to be enjoying her reacquaintance with a motorcycle, but she was hovering so close to the edge of the cliff roads that when I peered out from the sidecar, my stomach lurched at the sight of our precarious position. She seemed determined to get us down to the city in the shortest possible time, but she was leaving very little margin for error at that pace. We slipped and slid across the dirt, offering as little purchase as ice. Christa's skillful descent was akin to a medal-winning ice skater. I hoped that medal was gold because anything less than the best would see us reaching the bottom of this cliff far quicker than intended.

From time to time, I looked back and saw Gabriel's strained face under his helmet. I was sitting on his lap, tucked under a coarse, woolen blanket that smelt of dog. This must have been Bruno's bedding when he sat in the motorbike sidecar. The thought of Bruno alone in the jungle after Huggins's consumption induced a pang of guilt in the pit of my gut.

It then occurred to me that I hadn't eaten all day and was starving. The thought of food made me think of the breakfasts Aliba used to prepare for me at dawn, and the remorse in my core turned to anguish. My mother Aliba lost to the forest, Nishpunk and Bruno cowering in the shadows of the jungle, Huggins about to be roasted at a monkey barbecue. Every step I took seemed to cause loss to another. My selfish decisions caused harm to everyone around me. The most current people with something to lose were Christa and Gabriel. What peril was concealed behind the circus in the city?

My thoughts were plagued by the bitterest of emotions. Sadness, regret, anger, guilt, and despondency. I was not sure if my sanity could withstand another significant disappointment. Similar to the danger of navigating that winding motorcycle path, my mind was at the precipice and extremely close to falling into the abyss.

The lack of food added to the worries that consumed my conscience and mind. My eyes struggled with the sunlight and the rapidly disappearing road ahead. The jungle seemed to be dismissing me from its bosom and sending me into the outside world. I felt detached from the place I had come to know but never accepted. Were the confines of this environment ever my true home? Was that place real or just a figment of my imagination? Sleep was necessary, and to conserve energy, I rested my head on Gabriel's knee and pulled the blanket over my head.

I struggled to slip into rest, as my ears could not ignore the growling of the motorbike. I remembered that I used to say a prayer before sleep when I was a boy. I thought of my family and wished for their safety. However, this was not a prayer, as I was not asking a divine force to safeguard my loved ones. I was transmitting positive thoughts toward those special to me and hoped the message reached them in good spirits.

I thanked my parents for offering me a stable and loving childhood that enabled me to become the person I had become. I sent my love to my oldest brother, his wife, their daughter, my middle brother, and his wife and wished them good luck. I can no longer remember their names, but I can remember their love for me. The only name I could recall was Ashley's, and I hoped wherever she was, she had been able to mourn me and move on with her life. I wished this for all my family because, even though I was still alive in another form, they were unaware of it. I hoped they had not been irreparably damaged by my death. Sleep began to take hold as I considered this thought. *Why would they have been irreparably damaged? What did I do to them before I died?*

● ● ●

As soon as I fall asleep, I enter a dream world and stagger on my first step. You know the feeling when you step into a dream, look down, and realize there is nothing supporting your footing? As you miss your step, you immediately wake expecting a fall but realize you are lying asleep somewhere. I realize I am under the blanket and pull the cover from my eyes.

I am aghast and frozen with fear at the sight of an empty sidecar and the motorbike hurtling toward my doom. There is no time to think. Christa and Gabriel are gone, so I leap onto the handlebars. I am too small and weak to change the bike's trajectory, and it flies over the edge. I hurtle toward the abyss and scream in horror. I close my eyes and wait for the impact. Perhaps I will faint from the emotional shock incurred by the realization of my imminent demise. I hope my mind blanks out and I am not aware of a punishing collision or a lengthy, painful death. The wind passes through the fur on my face, and it actually feels quite comforting. I feel relaxed even though I am in mortal danger.

"What are you doing? Really enjoying the fan, I see."

The unmistakable voice of my Turkish lover. I open my eyes and find myself sitting in her car with the fan on full blast, aimed at my face. I look to my right, and there she sits, sweating in the summer heat of my past and smiling at my puzzled expression. The first thing I notice is her green eyes glowing in the seasonal sunshine. Typically, her eyes have a chocolate brown tinge, but at this moment, they shine like miniature, circular emeralds.

A film of sweat glistens on her forehead. The skin on her arms and shoulders is red due to a bit of sunburn. She may have Turkish blood, but she burns in the afternoon sunshine and never listens to my recommendation of shade. Her hereditary light skin from her father is aligned with a remarkably stubborn Mediterranean streak from her mother.

I cough and say, "Watch the road! don't look at me!" I take a moment to look around the car, which is full of all my possessions. It is the day we moved in together and are driving to her flat. We have been a couple for a few years and decided it was time to live together

She leans over and asks, "Why so quiet? Not getting cold feet are you?"

I sift back through my memories and can remember being worried and unsure of our future together. Yes, I wanted to live with Ashley, but I wasn't sure if this was the right time to settle down.

"No, baby. It is hot, and I feel a little claustrophobic with all this stuff. Also, I have socks on, so how could I get cold feet?" It's astonishing how pathetic I sound in hindsight. I sound like a cowardly moron. Claustrophobic is the word. I was a young man feeling throttled by responsibility and commitment. Why was I such an idiot? Why can't I tell her how I feel? It was natural to have reservations, but bottling up these worries was not good for anyone. I never wanted to disappoint her, but I should have been honest.

"Well," she says. "You can talk to me if you need to. I know this is a big step, but I love you and am so excited about living together."

I was filled with dread. It was strange because I recalled a faint memory of the sinking feeling associated with moving. Faint, because, looking at her now, I have a new perspective. If I could live this life again, I wouldn't be moody and unresponsive; I would rejoice at the opportunity to share my life with her.

The car comes to a halt, and she, again, makes a hash of parking in the space outside our flat. Number forty-eight Aberdeen Road, a small, one-bedroomed flat that anyone else would call cozy, but immediately reminded me of a cage.

The cage was a construction of my mind. My experiences as a monkey have meant actually spending time in a cage. *How could I ever have considered a home with Ashley to compare to being trapped?*

I reach over and put my hand on her shoulder. "Baby, I love you and am sure we will make this work."

In retrospect, I know these are hardly the most inspiring words for a partner. Women are extremely intuitive, and they can read between the lines. My wish was to paper over the cracks in our relationship, so I lean in for a kiss and close my eyes, waiting for her soft lips to connect with mine.

Physical communication can sometimes overpower unconvincing words. I wait for the kiss, but it doesn't come.

●●●

I opened my eyes and saw Gabriel's face. "Good dream, I gather? You have been making some very odd noises in your sleep. We even stopped and grabbed food, but you slept right through it."
Embarrassed, I withdrew my puckered lips and sat up.

We had left the forest behind and were on a tarmac road entering the urban jungle.

Gabriel tapped me on my head with a peeled banana, which I accepted gratefully. Seeing Ashley had infinitely increased morale, as it reminded me of the former life I was trying to salvage. Certain memories of my past life were so vivid that a part of me still believed I could return to my family, as ludicrous as that sounded.

Christa brought the bike to a halt by the side of the road and then shouted excitedly, "Look at that!"

At first, I did not know what she was referring to, but was thrilled when I saw directions to the circus. A wooden placard pointed to the right down a dirt path off the main road. The sign read *1 km to Circus*.

The placard was set against a broken-down, shabbily painted brick wall. The precariously standing wall had been painted white for a specific reason. The white paint was the background for a spray-painted threat. Beside the placard, a graffiti illustration had been created with some skill. Christa, Gabriel, and I stared at the message in silence.

Before us, a noose in black paint was wrapped around the throat of what was unmistakably a brown-colored monkey. Below the image were the words,

Welcome, Branko. We have been hanging around for so long, waiting for you to come and play.

28
PINK PANTS AND STRAIGHT JACKETS

I have never been one to back down from a challenge, and there was no time to lose. Whatever was waiting for me in this circus had been waiting long enough to draw a picture of my planned murder.

Gabriel and Christa looked down at me and immediately understood that the powers of fate were determining a necessary course. When confronted by threatening graffiti, we all knew our unavoidable path was towards peril. It occurred to me that this journey was mine to tread, and it was not necessary or advisable for my companions to continue with me.

Still, despite the welcome we had received, I knew my friends would not abandon me. I had to find a way to explain to them that this was a quest that I had to brave alone. We moved together for the moment, so I pointed at the big top down the dirt path.

The trail led straight in the direction of a yellow circus tent structure. No vegetation grew on the track leading to the structure. It was as if the pathway was not capable of supporting plants and instead negated life. You could call it a death path if you were so morbidly inclined.

The yellow tent seemed much more luminous at a distance, but as we approached, the shabby state of the outer material became more obvious. The yellow was stained with the unmistakable brown of aging and patches of green mildew. Rats scattered from around the entrance as we approached. A sign stood outside the opening that read, *Humans shall not enter. So please, Branko, tell your friends to stay out, or we'll cut out his vital organs and make her watch while we eat them.*

I turned toward my companions to see a visibly shaken Gabriel and Christa. My foster parents knew this was my battle and that whatever lay ahead was some kind of unquantifiable evil for me to overcome or succumb to alone. Christa knelt down with anguish etched across her face. I hugged her, and Gabriel joined our embrace. He defiantly stated, "We will wait out here for one hour. If you haven't returned, we will come in after you. I lost one boy. I can't lose another."

I leaped onto the ground and pointed at the sign outside the entrance. With my finger, I jabbed vigorously and repeatedly at the words, Humans shall not enter, and looked sorrowfully at them. I put my hand to my chest, then placed two fingers on my lips and sent each of them a kiss. That may be the last time I saw them, so I stared intently and inhaled their images. They were the only reason I had made it that far. I owed them my life. I owed them more than I can ever repay.

I turned to enter the tent, but as I took my first step, my legs wobbled at the knee, and I felt unsteady. I lost my footing and staggered to the floor. Christa ran to support me and helped me to my feet. My surroundings went dark, and I felt a sudden sharp pain in my chest. The monkey in me cried in reaction to the sharp jolt that shook my heart.

I grabbed at the closest thing to me, which was Christa's arm. I screamed again at what felt like a hand that entered my chest and was squeezing my heart with the intensity of a vice. Just before I fainted, the pain subsided; just as quickly as it overcame me, it vanished. Like a wave had crashed over me and imbalanced my equilibrium, I now found myself resting on the shore with a slightly dazed expression.

I looked beside me to see Christa with a gaping slash in her arm, profusely losing blood. Gabriel was making a makeshift tourniquet from a handkerchief, and I was aware another person had been seriously injured in my presence. If I didn't get away from Gabriel and Christa immediately, they would be the next to be killed. I raised myself and seemed to feel no pain; in fact, I was totally numb. Gabriel's stare caught mine, and I could see his face expressing a mixture of shock, worry, and sadness. For my friends' survival, I had to escape them. Their lives depended on it.

I sprinted toward the tent's entrance and leaped through the cloth door, bursting into blackness and dust. Immediately, I was aware that the air density within this place was much thicker than usual, and my nostrils were overcome by the sweet smell of candyfloss. The air became so syrupy it felt like I was walking through honey. The air's viscosity made it difficult to continue my forward momentum.

As my pupils adjusted to the obscurity, I began to see words written all around me on the walls, ground, and ceiling. Some sort of glow-in-the-dark substance was making different phrases light up at different moments in various corners of the room. I had to spin around to catch each message, and they didn't make for encouraging reading.

Whatever was waiting for me wanted to petrify me and was doing a very good job.

"You are going to die, monkey boy."

"Is it the past? Is it the present? Is it the future?"

"No Buddha to save you now!"

"Couldn't save your daddy? Couldn't save your mummy?"

"Time is running out."

"You don't even know your own name, but I do..."

"Time for you to see your skeletons."

"Relive nightmares and witness the lives you've destroyed."

"I will eat your pitiful boymonkey heart."

"You're a coward and deserve to die." I sensed a presence in the gloom as I read this last statement. I heard deep wheezing and felt a warm, damp breath on my neck. I spun around to face my tormentor, but no enemy lay before me.

Instead, I saw an arrow drawn in the same glowing paint, pointing at footprints left on the floor. I hurried along the path following the prints and was happy to move on from that dark room.

Spotlights outlined a corridor and a route through the tent. As I approached, I realized there was a terrifying scene lit under each shining bulb. Specifically, each stage had been set up with a taxidermically stuffed corpse of a primate. First, a monkey sitting in the lotus position with a finger up his nose. Then, an orangutan in a suit strangling himself with his own tie. Next, a grotesque stuffed gorilla in a tutu pirouetting and smiling maniacally. These were truly disgusting abominations against nature. Suddenly, the corridor went black and was then magically illuminated by a single light at the end of the narrow pathway.

Can it be? I hadn't seen that face in some time, but you never forget your own face. A stuffed body and head that almost exactly resembled my human form stood under the bright artificial light. I say *almost*, but it was me. I looked deranged and had a wild expression. The only clothes on my body were a fastened straight jacket and a pair of pink pants. A rope was wound around my waist as I sat on the floor. The rope led into the air and was attached to an overhanging wooden girder.

Dangling from the end of the rope was a monkey that was unmistakably also me, but in the form of Branko. The rope had broken my monkey neck, and my body hung limp and lifeless.

The sight seemed so real and yet so surreal, and it threw my mind into chaos. *Have I lost my sanity?* I fell to the floor and gasped for a breath of air that could cure my mental disorder. I could taste only bile in my mouth. I felt the same presence all around me, lurking and waiting to pounce.

"Come on then, if you want to eat my heart, come and face me and take it from my chest while it still beats." As soon as I said it, I regretted the words.

My tormentor appeared.

29
THE DWIDGET

nother spotlight lit in the distance. My surroundings were black, cavernous, and empty apart from one circular beam of light that streamed down onto a diminutive figure to my left. The thing in the light was difficult to make out, but it seemed to be scuttling on the floor. The inside of the tent was impossibly large, as the beam of light was at least a football field away. The illumination came divinely from above, and the indistinguishable person below was approaching.

I didn't dare move, but not out of fright. I wanted the light to reach me if it meant a tangible answer. Therefore, it wasn't necessary to rush toward my destiny. My fate approached, and I would become enlightened sooner or later.

Life had become quite surreal (a massive understatement), what with monkey dances, telepathic pigs, and human barbecues.

"What's the worst that could happen in a circus?" I shouted defiantly and realized my inner monologue had become an outer one. The light extinguished, and I stood alone in the familiar company of darkness. *Ich bin dunkel.* I am dark. *Hey, I speak German!*

Something brushed against my shoulder, and as I turned my head, a voice answered the question.

"Yes, you speak German. Kudos on getting here. I didn't think you would make it. Your path has been so incompetent that it almost seems you don't want to uncover the truth."

I lurched forward from the touch and the sound of the unfamiliar voice and suddenly felt a pang of sickness in the depths of my stomach. It was akin to the first turn of your intestines when you realize you have food poisoning. I could sense my brain's instinct to vomit and other neural pathways telling me to get away from whatever was beside me.

What was this monstrosity? I could barely see it, but it was so inherently vile that it induced nausea from the slightest touch.

My eyes refocused, and I saw the entity that could potentially explain my purpose in this world. There it was before me, a creature barely taller than my monkey frame, dirty, hairy, and pointing a crooked finger with a talon-like nail straight at my face. For a moment, it seemed as if a warped mirror had been placed in front of me. *Is this some sort of circus illusion to confuse me?*

However, no reflection-contorting glass could create this devilish dwarf before me. As the goblin became clear in my vision, I saw it was covered in hundreds of tiny pimples and pustules.

In a dismissive and disgusted tone, I questioned the deformity, "What are you, dwarf?"

Why did I find it necessary to ask such unnecessary questions in such a rude manner?

The dwarf continued to point his long, yellow nail toward me, then curled his top lip, raised his hooked nose, and snarled. He didn't seem like the friendliest critter. Perhaps he was actually a midget and was irritated by my presumptuous question. I was always confused as to the differentiation between a midget and a dwarf but, I must confess, it wasn't my top priority to ask this brute which clan he represented. Midget, dwarf, or perhaps a Dwidget?

The Dwidget screamed in indecipherable rage.

"Bbbbbbbblllllllllllllaaaaaaaaarrrrrggggghhhhhhhh!"

This communication wasn't going well. As it opened its mouth with impossible dexterity like an anaconda, I could see the uneven and broken teeth exposed by its roar. The arrangement of his top teeth looked like a familiar partly eroded coastal rock formation, perhaps Old Harry Rocks in the Jurassic Coast. At seeing the inside of his mouth, I had the urge to obtain a hammer just to smash those broken teeth out from its blackened gums.

I could sense the creature preparing to attack, although this wasn't due to some soothsaying ability. The giveaway signs were stamping his feet and drawing his left foot against the floor, building momentum like a tiny bull. The grunts and whines of this absurd minibeast meant I had to intervene to slow his intentions.

"Look Dwidget, before we battle, is there any chance we can discuss why I am here?"

The Dwidget froze, and I contemplated his grotesque, perplexed face and realized he was wearing a dark blue t-shirt that had been turned into a makeshift dress. The picture on the front of the shirt was of Nelson Mandela. I immediately recalled wearing that item of clothing in Parliament Square on the day Mandela visited London in 1996. That was *my* t-shirt. The little monster had stolen it and turned it into a dress!

"Where did you get my shirt from? Why have you brought me here? Please tell me what is going on!"

As the Dwidget spoke, my dislike for him increased disproportionately. The manner of his speech was irritating and his nasal voice grated. "You really don't know…" As he snorted a giggle, simultaneously, thick sputum escaped from his mouth, and a snot bubble inflated from his left nostril and popped. "You brought us to this place between life and death but can't deal with your consequences. I am your consequences… and now… only one of us can live."

The comment didn't make sense, but that seemed to be a continuing theme of my life.

30
NO GOLD AT THE END OF THIS RAINBOW

Branko was uneasy in the presence of the Dwidget. Perhaps it was the creature's chubby fingers attached to small hands at the ends of unusually muscular forearms. The thing's arms were much longer than his body required. In fact, they were so malformed that his arms almost looked as long as the stumpy legs hiding under his rotund belly. It was difficult to be sure because the true size of his belly was hidden by the Mandela dress.

The Dwidget's face was equally disproportionate, with minute ears at slightly different levels on the side of its head. The left ear was higher than the right, and between them was a bent nose with flared nostrils. The dark brown eyes of the creature were permanently wide open and seemingly stuck in a startled expression. In this lack of natural light, I couldn't tell if the miniman was covered in filth or if his pigment was actually dark brown.

As much as the Dwidget repulsed me, something about him encouraged restraint. Rather than be revolted by his unsightly appearance, I felt pity for him.

My ma used to say, "Never judge the man in the gutter because under different circumstances, that might have been you." What real control do we have over fate? Did my actions lead me to this situation, or was it a matter of me following the predestined flow of destiny?

I decided to change tack. "What is your name, friend?"

The Dwidget cackled with glee and retorted, "You really *are* stupid, aren't you, monkey boy? What with your poems and your religion. Look what you became, and look at me! I am a man, and you are nothing but a disgusting animal!"

My restraint towards the Dwidget was wearing thin.

He continued his tirade, "You killed your *daddy*." The Dwidget said *daddy* in a babyish manner. It was as if he was trying to provoke me.

The vocabulary stream of bile erupted from his mouth like a torrent of effluent from a broken gutter pipe. "You killed Aliba, too. Those two outside will be next. After I am done with you."

Unable to control my wrath, I unleashed my fury at the Dwidget, "Leave them out of this, you vile, wretched, minuscule, spotty little rat!"

The Dwidget smiled in an unsettling manner, apparently pleased that it had goaded me into losing control. "Good. Let the anger out, and you will prove how similar we are!"

As my pent-up resentment escaped, I felt a little light-headed. It was as if I was floating and I'd lost control of my senses. I almost felt like I was having an out-of-body experience and that I could see the Dwidget screaming abuse at Branko from outside my monkey carcass.

The evil released from the Dwidget wasn't spent, "Left your family to rot. Abandoned them., you did. Abandoned them! Only care for yourself. Never cared for them. Call me a rat, but you did truly terrible things."

Confused and disorientated, I blinked repeatedly and became one with Branko again, with my vision returning to a first-person perspective, staring at the Dwidget. This retched nanus could sense my weakness and sought to obfuscate me. I pleaded with it to speak sense, "Dwidget, rather than speaking in riddles, tell me the truth. What do you know? How did I come to be here? Answer me!"

The Dwidget's presence provoked a new emotion in me. It was as if his very aroma could aggravate me. I was unsure what spell he'd cast on me, but my deepest resentment was now unlocked. Something snapped to the extent I could actually hear the popping sound of my restraint.

The months of being in limbo between worlds had finally pushed me over the edge. The anger of an enraged primate and a boy on the edge of sanity were unleashed simultaneously. I ran at the stumpy-legged creature and jumped on him. He laughed at my attack, cackling as I throttled him. He croaked with delight as I attempted to squeeze the last drop of breath from his lungs. As I pressed on his skin, pimples burst under the pressure of my fingers, unleashing blood and pus, and the bloody yellow scum clung to my fingers and thumbs.

I treated his neck like a moist sponge that I had to squeeze dry. However, a strange dizziness came over me as I continued to strangle the spotty beast. Sparks flew in my vision, and I saw stars and white light all around me.

Rather than looking down at the Dwidget, I was again above my body, looking down at Branko and the creature. I saw Branko relinquish his hold, and the Dwidget take me by the throat. The Dwidget looked up at me, floating from my vantage point, and let out a short, vengeful laugh.

As he snickered, he addressed me, "Fell right into my trap, you did. You are at your weakest when angry, but now for the final straw. You see, now you must know who you are. There are a few things you will soon know. This is the first."

Rather than respond, I remained quiet. To be honest, I wasn't sure if I would be able to address the Dwidget while having an out-of-body experience. I felt as detached as a prosthetic limb.

"Do you want to know your former name?"

I nodded in astonishment. It seemed the grotesque circus freak before me had the answers I had been searching for.

The Dwidget took the arms of my monkey body and began dancing a ballroom step with my ragdoll shell. He was performing what appeared to be a dramatic and intimate tango in silence whilst staring into Branko's eyes. The performance was both hideous and startling in equal measure.

"Absolutely no idea lost!" he danced as he screamed the words into my lifeless face.

I had to calm down and regain control of this situation. He said I was playing into his hands with my rage, so I needed to relax. I refocused on the scene below me. There was something absurd about seeing a vertically challenged abomination doing what now appeared to be the foxtrot with the body of a monkey—which happened to be me. This was like the dream of an unhinged mental patient.

I went to my happy place and controlled my breathing. My mind was transported to a distant world where Ashley and I sat by a beach in a beautiful place called Pasikuda, northwest of Sri Lanka. I thought of the waves hitting the shore and the cheerful chirp of the friendly, anonymous birds. I remembered holding her hand as I sipped on a freshly opened coconut in a world that was impossibly perfect compared to this place.

The Dwidget dragged me back to reality with his continued stream of drivel. "Come on, monkey fool! Here is another one. You are a nincompoop imbecile loser!"

Don't concentrate on the babble of this lunatic. I tried to focus my mind. *Be calm and stop him from defiling your body with that awful tango.*

The Dwidget's gibberish was never-ending, "Anger negates introspective learning! Oh, that was a good on! Come on, nincompoop. Solve the riddle and figure out who you are!"

I continued my breathing exercises. Deep inhalation, deep exhalation. In, out. In, out.

The Dwidget roared with annoyance, "*Stop that deep breathing!* You look like a pregnant woman! Okay, let's see if you get *this one*. Analysis needed in language!" When I didn't respond, he shouted, "Come on, you aren't even trying! And that was an easy one. You really are stupid. I always was the brains!"

His comment gained my attention. He had referred to us as one on numerous occasions. I took a deep breath and found myself staring into the Dwidget's eyes as we spun around the dim circus tent. "How do we know each other?" I asked.

As we twirled, the Dwidget sang in a horrific tone-deaf tune, "First things first, monkeyfaceman. First, you figure out who you are, and *then* I tell you how we know one another. *A needle in limbo! All nonsense is logic!*"

The answer hit me like a punch to the face. The truth was—and had been—evident all along. I remembered who I was, yet the name I had been searching for did not give me the relief I expected. *What is in a name?* Finding my name wasn't the gold at the end of the rainbow as I had hoped.

"Okay, let me try one," I interrupted and then shouted, *"Avoid nasty insidious little Dwidgets!"*

The Dwidget immediately stopped his mad march and confirmed I had solved the puzzle. "Actually, you got that one wrong."

I was overcome with an utterly unexpected sadness at the realization of my past human identity, "I have figured out your riddle, Dwidget. I know my name. My name is the first letter of the words in all your sentences. My name is... my name was *Anil.*"

Remembering who I was suddenly made me realize how far I had traveled away from that person.

31
SOME TRUTHS ARE DIFFICULT TO SWALLOW

My name, which I have been searching for in this preposterous world, was Anil. Not that exciting in the end. I was hoping for Isambard Kingdom, Gorilla Monsoon, or even Nelson Muhammad Bruce Lee. However, Anil is who I was, and although it didn't fill me with elation, it fit like an old sweater with a hole in the armpit.

My name was Anil, but the question was, *what good would my name do me here?* Another strange thought entered my consciousness, the fact that Branko and I were no longer one but merely two companions sharing the same elevator, unsure if we were going up or plummeting to earth.

Throughout our journey so far, we had been a unified entity, rejoicing in the few successes we shared and desperately mourning the losses that had become all too frequent. Now we were two entities, and I felt we might never be united again. I had taken this primate's body hostage and led him from the safety of the jungle. I had contributed to his mother being killed and exposed his young mind to mind-altering visions that would have broken a weaker individual. He and I had survived this hellish world until now, but I was unsure if we would be able to maintain our good fortune.

I came out of my stupor and stared at my tiny nemesis. I decided I had been too reactive to this cunning little creature and had to try to cajole him through this negotiation. "So, Dwidget. I know my name, but you told me there was more to this riddle. You said you could provide me with the answers."

The Dwidget replied incredulously, "Haven't you realized? You fool! Stupid monkey-brained idiot. You weren't that clever as a human and appear to be even more dumb as a monkey. Actually, I guess that makes sense."

Just being near the Dwidget raised my ire again. I couldn't understand why he provoked such vexation within me. I felt drawn to him and repelled by him simultaneously. We were like magnets whose polarity kept switching. At this moment, I wanted to get close enough to crush him, but he was a spritely fellow, and as I approached, he seemed to read my thoughts and, just at the right time, avoided my grasp.

The Dwidget raised his dukes like a little prize fighter and began throwing little punches my way. He was hopping around the floor in front of me. "Okay, Anil. Or should I call you Branko? Who are you exactly? Actually, you are both and neither. The next thing you should know is why you are here. Would you like to know that? What do you think of my boxing? Do you remember you used to box? You thought you were quite good but spent most of your time getting beaten up." Smiling, the Dwidget knew he had my full attention. I sat, submissively staring at his wonky smile's broken, yellow teeth. His boxing reminded me that I had boxed a bit in my youth and, unfortunately, he was right. I spent more time being hit than hitting others!

The Dwidget continued to shadow box around my periphery, just out of reach of my grip. He was luring me to a conclusion that I knew I had to hear but didn't want to. He abruptly stopped his aggressive punching and stared right into me. Then he ominously said, "Unfortunately, the tales I have to tell are nightmarish, my old friend. I am not the sort of creature who tells stories with a happy ending."

I simply nodded from my vantage point on the floor. I waited for his narrative to start while remembering memories of happier times. My mind flitted from this ghoulish reality to flickers of euphoria in my past. Playing with Ava on her swing in the garden and hearing her squeal with delight each time I pushed her. Happy thoughts kept me calm in this woeful place. As the Dwidget drew closer and sat before me, the darkness in the room became impenetrable. There was no escape from whatever the Dwidget had to reveal. I had to embrace whatever truth he had to give.

The creature sat in the lotus position before me and stuck a dirty finger with a sharp nail up his right nostril. I sneered at his disgusting manners and leaned away from his filth.

The Dwidget quickly retorted to defend himself against my revulsion, "You use the same sticks to eat termites with as you put up your bum and yet have the nerve to turn your nose up at me?"

I suppose he had a point. Perhaps we weren't that different at all. He pulled some sort of sticky, brown, and green obstruction from his nostril and took a deep breath whilst simultaneously sucking all the snot into his mouth. He then viciously spat the concoction onto the ground to make it clear he was ready to unleash the big finale. It was obvious he had waited an eternity to tell this story. The cleared nostril made a faint whistling sound as he exhaled.

Locking into my gaze, he took a deep breath and emitted a volcanic release of gas. It was a fart that could be heard around the world. I pleaded with this monstrosity to stop wasting my time, but as I did so, I was overcome by the noxious gas. I coughed uncontrollably, and my eyes teared up such that I could no longer see the Dwidget in front of me. I closed my eyes and kneeled on the floor. I was then overcome by the creature's voice all around me, as if he were speaking to me on a jacked-up speaker system set to maximum volume.

He began. "So, you used to be a student in London. I gather you remember this much."

From my contorted and blinded position on the floor, I replied, "Yes, and I died and somehow came to this place. Some sort of accident occurred. I can't remember the details."

I continued to listen with my eyes closed. The Dwidget laughed, "An accident? Hahahahaha!" cackled the deviant, laughing at my ignorance. "First things first—do you remember Ashley?"

How did the Dwidget know so much about me? I gave him the confirmation he desired, "Yes, she was my girlfriend, a Turkish girl with brown eyes that turned green in the—" the Dwidget spat on the floor to swiftly interrupt me. "I get it, you remember her. Green eyes and a face like the morning sunshine. Well, the reason you are here is because of her!"

"That doesn't make any sense. How can she be the reason?"

"Shut up, monkey bitch, and you might hear the end of the story. You were a student in London. Quite successful, too. Clever young chap, making waves, with huge potential. But although you seemed confident, the opposite was true. Quite popular with people but not a success. You used to second guess yourself, always questioning whether you were making the right decisions. Then she came into your life. Amazing, really, why someone like her choose someone as worthless as yourself? Well, that was the spark, not just in your romance but in your whole life. Suddenly, this guy who had never experienced love outside of family felt he could take on the world."

"So, I became a success. What does that have to do with me being here?"

"***Shut up and listen!*** You were a different person back then: relaxed but without drive, passionate but with no determination, going through the motions and never fulfilling your potential. But then she came into your life, and suddenly, your ego exploded. You forgot the person you were and tried to become something stronger, more powerful, *hungrier*. You were no longer the poor little boy who lost his daddy. No longer the weakling who needed Ashley's support."

There was something in the glint in the Dwidget's eye that made me not want to hear the rest of this story. Something within him was savoring telling me these home truths.

"A few years of confidence and you began to forget about her. She was so trusting; why would she believe you had changed, that you had become something new, something everyone wanted, not just someone she loved? There is nothing worse than someone who takes advantage of another person's trust."

Memories slowly came back to me, and strange feelings glimmered in my mind. I concentrated on them and could no longer hear the Dwidget's drone or nose whistle. A name seeped into my thoughts. It seemed so familiar, a name that led me to the jungle.

I coughed out the word so quietly it almost couldn't be heard. "Rachel."

"So, the monkey remembers Rachel. Strange, isn't it? Up to this point, you could only remember Ashley's name. What about your *other* lover?"

It can't be true! I thought, yet immediately, I knew the Dwidget's testimony was correct. I had spent time away from Ashley and got close to someone else on my course at university.

"Do you remember what happened next, Anil?"

I shook my head, more in the hope that he would stop rather than in response to his question. I knew where this road was heading. We were heading off a cliff into the most profound guilt of my past. The feelings I had been repressing for these months in the jungle.

The malignancy within the Dwidget was renewed with every word he uttered, "Well, Anil, not only were you seeing Rachel, but you were also quite a proficient drinker. It seems the only way you could suppress your guilt was with alcohol. You were a real slimeball. Cheating on the only person who ever chose to love you, the person whose love made you. You were nothing, and then your ego grew out of control. The negativity that grew within you diminished any light from your original love… and that's where *I* come in."

My eyes opened, and the Dwidget reappeared, tottering toward me with a large square object balanced on his head, held in place with his arms. He placed the item before me, a square mirror showing a warped reflection. The sort of mirror you would see in a funhouse. "You want to know who we are?" He stepped beside me into the reflection of the mirror.

He stood before me, so half of his body and half of mine showed in the reflection. I stared with astonishment. The mirror no longer reflected either of us but now showed my former self, Anil Perera.

I looked down at the creature in shock but also in realization. "You are part of me, Dwidget? You are some lost part of my identity, of my… soul?"

My other half began weeping tears of sorrow, and I felt sadness for its suffering.

He cried mournfully, "At first, I was a small flea, screaming to get your attention in the vast empty cave that is your mind. I was birthed from within you after you lost your father. A small seedling of hatred that just needed the right circumstances to blossom. Then I noticed your behavior started to change. You decided to be more ruthless and forget about the people who made you who you were. Your personality changed to allow you to reach new expectations. I am the cancer in you that ate all the anger, that fuelled your desire, that drank and consumed and hated anything in your path. I am the creature you had to create within yourself to be a success."

The world spun out of control, and my stomach felt loose. Vomit spewed from my mouth like a detonation, emptying any remaining contents.

I cleaned the bile from around my mouth and desperately lamented, "But why? Why the change in me? Why did I suddenly hate?"

The Dwidget whined in a tone that made me irate, "Because you are weak and because your daddy died, and it gave you an excuse!"

At this comment, I leaped at the creature, but it was as if his mind was one step ahead of me, and he side-stepped, disappearing. I felt a murderous intent and wanted to kill him, to end this disgusting growth, but how do you execute the worst part of you? The voice of immoral decisions will always be in us. I needed the strength and willpower to withstand that malignancy.

I screamed into the darkness, "*Come and face me, Dwidget!*"

Hidden away, the creature's reply echoed, "Before you attack me, foolish Anil, remember, you have not heard the end of the story. You had become an abomination, but that doesn't explain why you are here. Do you want to know? Of course, you do and *I want to tell it.*"

His nasal voice resonated all around me and penetrated my very core.

"That nasal voice is *your* voice, idiot!" the Dwidget said with a laugh. "It sounds different when you are on the outside, doesn't it? But about your demise—

"You embarked on your affair. Rachel didn't want it to be just a fling. She wanted the whole package, so she informed Ashley of what had been happening for months behind her back. Unfortunately for you, she told Ashley on the remembrance day of your dad's death anniversary."

I suddenly knew the hideous end to this tragedy and desperately didn't want to hear the conclusion. I covered my ears and kneeled on the floor, hoping for mercy.

The Dwidget chuckled as his nose whistled. "No. No, my brother Brankanil, you will hear this to the end. You will receive no mercy from me. This is what you have been searching for, and now you will consume every last word. You came home, drunk, drowning in your sorrow and feeling sorry for yourself. Why you were sad, I don't know. You got a few pennies from the old man when he popped it—you should have been glad!"

My hatred for my other half was at the boiling point. He knew my every weakness. The accusations he threw at me were like someone putting a needle through my eye, although I felt excruciating pain all over my body, in my eyes, my neck, and my heart. The pain I felt wasn't from the Dwidget's words but my own guilt, which riddled my body like a disease.

The Dwidget now whispered the climax to his tale: "Ashley asked you if it was true, and you said it was. At least at this point, you did the honest thing and admitted your deceit. She cried and pleaded for an explanation. You told her you didn't want to discuss the matter on such a day. However, that wasn't going to suffice in this situation. You walked out of the house and tried to get into her car. The rain was pouring, so when you looked back at her face, you couldn't tell if the water beneath her eyes was rain or tears. She chased you and got into the car, telling you not to run away because you were drunk and could hurt yourself. She pleaded with you to stay and talk, to figure things out, but you were out of control by then. You started the car and drove into the night. Visibility was nil, and you were going much too fast in those conditions. A collision was inevitable, and someone was going to get hurt... and they did."

I hoped that would be the end, but was sure this disaster had a fitting outcome.

"You're right—we're not done yet, monkeyman. This part *really* gets my juices flowing! You crashed the car, but it was a minor crash for you. The car slipped off the road and hit a lamp post on the *passenger* side, *Ashley's* side. The impact sobered you instantly, and you called an ambulance. On arriving at the hospital, Ashley was rushed into the operating theater. It seemed her internal injuries were more complicated than first thought. You waited outside the operating room without reporting to anyone what had occurred that night. Finally, a doctor approached you to report on Ashley's health. Do you want me to finish?"

I had to know what I did and pleaded with this monster, "Tell me, Dwidget… I have to hear the truth."

"The doctor told you that Ashley would be fine but that her pregnancy had ended. She was three months along. You killed your own baby, a child you weren't even aware of."

There was no substance left inside me, leaving the nausea no release. I felt like this news was about to induce another out-of-body experience. I couldn't breathe or move, and my thoughts descended into oblivion. I had destroyed both my and Ashley's lives.

My spiritual cancer reappeared before me, rubbing himself with glee, overcome by the ecstasy of the moment. "The final piece of the jigsaw is at eleven twenty-three pm, on the fourteenth of May, on the three-year anniversary of your father's death. You jumped off the Waterloo Bridge. And *that* is how you and Branko came to be."

This last piece of information broke my weary conscience. My route to Branko was suicide. I had lost the will to survive and killed myself.

32
WHO TO TRUST?

The Dwidget fled and continued to taunt me from afar. "Killed yourself! Killed yourself! Disgusting, pathetic coward who gave up on himself! Buddha laughing at the disgraced scum, demoted to a monkey! Reincarnation is a fine thing if you live a good life. Dirty human wannabe filth, putrid monkey mess!"

Every piece of abuse that the Dwidget threw at me caused yet more pain. His insults seemed to have a physical resonance that struck every nerve in my body. Each insult made me feel weaker and targeted at my innermost vulnerability.

"Thought you might go home, didn't you, monkeyfool? No way for you to go home! Why don't you end your pitiful existence now and finally rid this world of your presence? Get it right this time. End your life for good!"

Perhaps he was right, and the end of my journey was to find the truth and let my soul rest. I stepped up, facing the warped mirror, looked at the sad monkey before me, and began crying self-pitying tears—which were surely the most pathetic kind. From what I have heard, I had no reason to feel sorry for myself. My brother Sidath told me I would have to face my past and take responsibility for my life, but was it just a figment of my imagination? What in this world was real? Could he have known I had killed my unborn child and almost killed my girlfriend? What redemption could I find from that tragedy?

I felt the tears leak from my eyes and fall onto my chest and arms. I was slumped forward and suddenly felt a push on my left shoulder. In the reflection before me, Branko and I were no longer one. We sat beside each other and he was the one nudging me. He wanted to wrestle. I lashed my left arm in his direction, and he cowered back in fear. He paused in a crouch and watched me with trepidation before he skipped toward me and pushed my shoulder again.

I roared with rage in a way that was reminiscent of the disappeared Dwidget, *"Don't you understand? You stupid monkey! I have ruined everybody's lives! I* couldn't save my dad, I ruined my life, I destroyed Ashley's, and I killed... my child! *And I killed your mother!"*

With this statement Branko looked aghast, then hissed at me. I could see the wild fear of an animal's inability to comprehend. I was beyond caring about my monkey brother. Branko's naivety sickened me and made my fallibility even more manifest.

I swiped at my embarrassing primate relative, "Get away from me, you foolish monkey! ***Get away before I kill you, too!"***

Before I finished the sentence, he scuttled away into the shadows. The moment I said the words, I regretted them. Branko saved me from the darkness once before, and as he left me, I found myself alone in the bleak wilderness again.

The Dwidget had been spying from afar, and as I turned to find his hideous form, he rubbed his hands together with obvious satisfaction.

Dancing on the spot, he exclaimed, "You did it, Anil, you did it! You expelled the monkey! Now we can be one again. Now we can be one!"

The smile on the cancer's face made my guts lurch such that I could actually taste my guilt.

I burped out a question that had immediately popped into my mind: "What do you mean we can be one?"

The Dwidget was suddenly transformed into a sycophantic and servile form, "I wasn't totally honest with you, master, but I needed you to expel the monkey. You see, I needed to enrage you to bring you closer to me and allow our reunification."

His unending deceit brought forth an unprecedented fury, *"What weren't you honest about, Dwidget?"*

He cowered as he replied, "Don't be angry, master. You heard most of the details. After you jumped off the bridge, we were separated. Some sort of force wanted to keep you away from me. I searched the darkness and scoured the abyss looking for your being. Just before I could snare you, I saw that pitiful primate luring you to him, trying to replace me and join with your soul. But *we* are meant to be. You and I were one, and we shall be again!"

I was confused by his explanation. Why was he so desperate for us to be reunited after he told me he despised me and after I killed us?

Reading my thoughts, he answered the question in my head: "Well, master, perhaps that is where I stretched the truth the most—"

"Tell me now!"

"Perhaps master is not dead, and there is a way home."

The impact of this statement seemed to affect my hearing. My eardrums felt like they were in a vacuum, and I could no longer hear the Dwidget's words but could see he was still mouthing some sort of explanation.

Did he just tell me I was still alive?

I saw the Dwidget's crooked teeth and black rancid lips make the shapes of words but still couldn't hear a sound. Slowly, his voice came into range, and I heard, "Master, master, are you okay?" He was fawning over me, rubbing my human arms and back. "Can you hear me, master? I'm sorry to have lied to you, but this is as I understand it. Something separated us and left you in the Nothing. The monkey rescued you and this prevented us from reuniting. Now we can go back home, but three doesn't go into two. The monkey has to be eliminated for us to return to our family.

"The monkey has to die. You have to kill him."

33
THREE INTO TWO

The last sacrifice after endless amounts of sacrifice was that I must kill the only thing that had shown me any compassion or kindness in this bleak existence. Of course, fate would demand that Branko die before I return home. Even more shameful, that disgusting thing, the Dwidget, was a part of me.

Could the Dwidget be right? I have been lost in this jungle for so long that my mind struggled to comprehend this version of the truth. Three souls cannot inhabit my body. The Dwidget seemed to be some sort of necessary evil presence, a balance in the person that was Anil Perera. From what I have heard, I hated the person I became, and it caused me to try to commit suicide. However, it seemed as if the only means of returning to my family was by reuniting with the spiritual cancer that had ruined my life and made me into the thing I came to despise. My mind raced at the thought of executing my little friend. Why did Branko have to be eliminated? He was the best thing about me. Why couldn't he go on independently now that I have the chance to reform my soul?

The Dwidget continued his annoying habit of answering the unsaid questions in my grey matter: "Because he has become inherently part of you, master. When he saved you, his soul combined with yours. Now, to return to our family, he must die. Don't you want to go home? See your mummy, brothers… *Ashley?*"

I desperately wanted to go home, and that desire was stronger than any other thought in my mind or emotion in my heart.

The route back to my family had become tangible and so I asked what steps were required to go home, "How do we get rid of Branko?"

The Dwidget put his hands behind his back and informed me of his plan, "Oh master, I have the perfect weapon. If you lure him back to us, I can leap from the shadows and plunge this into his heart."

The Dwidget unleashed a small, razor-sharp dagger. His expertise with the silver-handled knife unsettled me as he manipulated it between his fingers.

Instinctively, I knew it had to be me to end the monkey. "I will handle the dagger. I will kill Branko. The monkey must die at my hand."

I watched as the Dwidget considered my offer. He stared into me as if reading my very intentions from the look on my face and the angle of my stance. Reluctantly, he hopped before me and offered the blade.

"I can read master's thoughts, so I am happy to let master be the slayer of the stupid monkey."

I accepted the dagger and immediately knew this knife offered me a route home. I had to clear my mind of guilt and concentrate on the objective. Whatever means necessary to get back home. *Whatever means necessary to get back to Ashley*. This will all be a distant echo of a nightmare that evaporated like a morning mist.

Three doesn't go into two, and someone must die. But how do I lure Branko back to me? I needed some sort of bait to encourage his return.

"Dwidget, I will call Branko. He will come to me if I lure him. However, to do this, I need some fruit. Bananas would be ideal. When the monkey comes to me, I want you to grab him so I can deliver the fatal blow."

"Master, once you have slain the monkey, be sure to hold onto me to enable our souls to fuse. I am not sure what will happen when we combine, but we will be delivered from the jungle, and we must travel together."

I called to Branko and waved my other half into a dim corner of the tent. My glance sideways caught the Dwidget as he scarpered, but when I glanced back at my feet, a bunch of bananas sat on the floor. They were perfectly ripe. I picked one up and began peeling and contemplating the horror ahead. I knew my thoughts must focus only on Branko's death. I had to build up to this pinnacle of tragedy as that was what was required to make it back to my family.

In my most dulcet tones, I called out to Branko, "Little brother, return to me. Brother monkey, please come back. I am sorry. I was angry. Come back, I have food for you."

Within seconds, I heard the patter of feet signaling Branko's return. He had no reason to distrust me, and I saw the eager anticipation in his eyes. I threw him a banana from the bunch, and he caught it with ease.

With Branko distracted by the treat, the Dwidget leaped from the shadows and landed on him. A scuffle ensued, and I heard the yelp of the Dwidget as Branko sank his teeth into his flesh. A blur of monkey fur and dwarf forearms rolled before my eyes and the screams of the demonic Dwidget alongside Branko's screeches combined to create a deafening effect. *I have to end this efficiently and ensure my journey home.*

The Dwidget managed to overcome the smaller baby monkey. "I have him subdued, master. Plunge the knife into him before he manages to break free!"

I approached the Dwidget, who was sitting on top of the forlorn monkey. I raised the knife above my head and stared into Branko's eyes. I saw tears mixed with fear, and he offered a last look of resignation. He was evidently amazed that his last remaining family was abandoning him.

At every step of this lunacy, I thought I had reached my nadir but now realized at this moment that I couldn't get any lower. "I am so sorry Branko. This is the only way I can return home."

My last lucid thought before committing murder was the clinical realization that I would always sacrifice another for my own survival. I had done that repeatedly in my past life, and it seemed I was destined to repeat it in my reincarnated life as a monkey.

The knife plunged through the thick, wet air, and just before the creature's death, I heard only one word: "Betrayed!"

Blood spurted from the wound and sprayed up like a fountain into my face. I was unable to see due to the force of release. The creature screamed, and the howls reverberated in my mind. The pain in my body seemed to be cutting a line through the center of me, as if I were being split in two. I pushed the hideously wounded body of the creature aside and saw the entity that would share my soul forever more.

I reached out and clung to the body of my balance in life. I hugged the small frame and felt the fusing of our essence. A white light blinded my vision, but I was comforted by the embrace with the soft fur of my monkey brother.

Three couldn't go into two, so one of us needed to die. The Dwidget was slain, and Branko took his place. But what would fate have in store for us next?

34
GUESS WHO IS IN MY CORNER

As I gripped Branko's little form, it felt as if we were melting together. Our bodies became entwined and fused, the pain of such a process elicited screaming and wailing in equal measure. Gravity had no impact as we hurtled through a familiar oblivion. We didn't fall down, but instead, we spun, fused, and transformed. Likely due to the disorientation that I was experiencing, I suddenly sought to hug Branko's body and realized he was no longer within my grasp. Had I lost him in our journey through the void?

A familiar smell permeated my nostrils, the smell of the impossible past. I hadn't smelled it in years, but I was so bewildered I could only assume my senses were playing tricks on me. My mind stopped revolving, and I realized my body was fixed on a flat surface. The scent was of a familiar aftershave mixed with the smoke of a cigarette, and it reminded me of hopeful, happier times. I was sitting in the darkness, and I was aware someone was facing me by the sound of their shallow inhalation of breath.

"Hello. It has been a long time." The stranger's voice was unfamiliar for a microsecond, but as my brain recollected that voice, the hairs on my arm immediately stood, and a surge of electricity ran through my spine.

A voice so soothing it was like sitting in a warm bath. A sound so calming that my world altered from chaos to tranquillity in an instant. The happiness that filled my heart made me feel as if I would burst. I was unable to utter any speech, scared a word spoken might fracture the nirvana I now inhabited, and worried this experience would be fleeting.

"You have been through a lot. I have been watching from afar but was unable to be involved. Until I realized you desperately needed my help. Coming here has meant overcoming almost insurmountable odds for both of us. Just being here is a miracle in itself. I needed to be with you. You must know death is a part of life. For some reason, you have been unable to learn this lesson. I died with dignity, surrounded by my family. That's all you can ever hope for. You were not to blame for my death or any of the deaths that have taken place. They are just a part of the cycle of our journey. However, that doesn't mean you haven't made mistakes in your life. Although you never let me down, you have let down those who needed you the most."

The shame of being confronted with the guilt of my past by this person made me glad I was hidden by the surrounding darkness.

I tried to croak out a response. My mind thought *I couldn't get past guilt, sadness, and self-pity. It consumed me*, but I was unable to utter a word.

"I understand your frailty, and this is why I am here today. We have a connection that can never be broken. I have been watching you since we were separated so long ago. I have seen your successes and your failures. Do you realize you were always a success in my eyes? Your anger corrupted you and misdirected you. The pain of loss polluted your judgment and desires. I taught you to live a life of purpose where your ambition should be to have integrity and make the right choices. My expectations of you were never complicated. You needed to experience purity and naivety in life to address your mistakes with a new perspective. You have the potential to be something great but have got lost en route. I have been trying to guide you along the right path. I have always been in your corner, attempting to gently push you in the right direction."

The madness of this moment was not lost on me. I didn't believe it could be true, so I just quietly listened and hoped it might never end. Before I became Branko, I was a person who believed in logic, and spirituality was a magic that I indulged as a childish fantasy. Yet, look where I found myself when following my instincts down a path that was impossible to explain.

"My death was not your fault. I was old, had drunk a little too much whiskey, and smoked a few too many cigarettes. I'd rather not see you smoking one again, if possible. It was my time to go, but it is not yours yet. However, meddling with fate's plan is a challenging process. There are powers in the universe that assist positive and negative outcomes. Something was determined to destroy you, and that entity influenced the growth of the evil presence inside you.

"I am merely an observer now, not meant to meaningfully influence your world. So, I watch and share all of your experiences. I spend most of my time keeping an eye on your mother. I watch her waking up in the morning, and sometimes, her first look is across to my side of the bed. For a few seconds, she forgets the reality that we are separated, and she is content. I then share her sinking realization that we are forever apart. I am cursed by the sadness etched on her face. I watch her sitting in the garden, remembering our time together, and sometimes her eyes fill with tears. She sorrowfully weeps for the past, and every tear that falls is a painful torture for me. I couldn't allow your death to cause her more pain. *You* have to protect your family… *You* have to survive…

"A power much greater than mine determines all our fates. Fortunately, that power also wanted to offer you a means of redemption. Another living presence of great purity also agreed you were worth saving; otherwise, I am unsure who else would have helped you.

"Branko was the vital element that allowed your survival. He was the yin to the evil that was present within you. Ultimately, he will sacrifice himself for you to remain. That is how much he loves you. He is a spirit guide. You are very fortunate an entity capable of such sympathy chose you, Anil. Branko loves you like a brother, but your original family needs you, too. Your family needs you to survive. Your mother and brothers need you to live. I can't allow my death to lead to your suicide, so I used whatever influence possible to direct you down the right path.

"You have one last chance, and time is scarce, but your journey is incomplete. For you to survive requires yet more tragedy. Remember my advice and choose the right path. There is a limited amount of time. I cannot give you all the answers, but know this—I will always be with you. Never feel alone again as I live inside your heart. When you tried to save me, your love and desire created a never-ending connection between us. I live on in you and all our family. I live on through you. I have moved heaven and earth to remind you how much I love you.

"I want to leave you with one last gift, as it were. We used to sing a Beatles song together when you were a child. You could never pronounce the actual lyrics, and it always made me laugh when you tried to sing it. I think you have been trying to remember, but you were so young when we sang together. *Bloody Bloodah!*"

I immediately blurted out the next line without thinking, "Life goes on." The song we sang when I was a child was *Obladi, Oblada,* and I suddenly recalled the times when I would scream the words together with my father.

I couldn't prevent responding as I did as a child and shouted in return the lyric from the song I cherished. It was the song that played in the ambulance that took my dad to the hospital on the day he died. It was a signal to me that life must go on and cannot stop even when one of the foundations of your being crumbles. That pillar leaving your life doesn't mean the whole infrastructure of your existence has to collapse.

There was silence in the darkness. I dared not move lest I unsettled the equilibrium. I would happily remain in this nothingness for eternity with that voice and scent to soothe me. But I was also sure that the presence would already be gone if I reached out. I raised my hand and pushed out, desperately hoping to be mistaken. The familiar soft skin of his hand touched mine for the briefest moment.

I knew I must offer one last apology. "I am sorry I let you down. I love you, old man." My statement was met with no response.

35
RIGHT PATH TO THE GLORY OF LOVE

I concentrate my mind on the conversation that has just passed. The ghost of my father, his soul from another dimension, a figment of my imagination, whatever you want to call it, said to choose the right path, but what is the right decision when you are sitting alone in the dark? I raise my right arm to my eyes, wipe away the tears, and consider my next move.

It occurs to me to take my father's advice literally. I roll to my right, and my weight opens a door. Then, I fall out onto a soft carpeted floor. There is daylight shining into a messy bedroom. I compose myself after the fall and try to focus on my surroundings. In front of me is a mirror, and the reflection facing me is Branko's. I am still a monkey, but now I am in the familiar surroundings of my former life.

Something about this scenario reminds me of the past, but I am unsure if it is fiction or reality. It feels as if not only have I been in this room before, but that I am experiencing déjà vu. An unknown entity stirs on the bed beside the mirror. I am not tall enough to see who is resting there, but am pretty sure I recognize enough of the objects in this room to make an educated guess. On the floor beneath the bed is a hockey stick and dirty sports kit. Sitting on the bookshelf are two books I used to own, *Kafka on the Shore* and *The Great Gatsby*. Two of my favorites that were loaned and never returned, but hopefully read. Besides the books, there is a picture of Ashley and Anil Perera sharing an embrace in a frozen image from our shared past.

Could she be above me, sleeping on this bed? Am I that close to a reunion? How on earth did my dad manage to get me back here? I jump onto the edge of the bed and see the back of her head, a mop of brown hair disheveled by sleep. I creep toward her, not wanting to break her rest and revel in her beauty.

I have watched her sleep so many times, but this time, I have a warning sense of trepidation. My sense of caution is overcome by the vision before me. As I look at her, the first rays of morning sun illuminate her. I can see speckles of eyeliner in her eyelashes. I am desperate to touch her again and forget my current circumstances. I stroke her face, and she smiles and rubs against me like a contented cat. As she rubs up against my body, some of my fur tickles her nose, and she sneezes.

I've experienced this before! I think in alarm. Just like in my dream many months ago, she wakes abruptly, and even her half-open eyes cannot hide her horror. She hurls herself away from me, screaming and lashing out with kicks and swipes of her arms.

I've lived this experience before but cannot change the chain of events.

I try to control her wildly swinging limbs, but she starts screaming hysterically. I try to speak, but only panic-fuelled cries escape my mouth. Women are so difficult to read. Ashley always said she wanted an animal in the bedroom, but perhaps this was not what she meant.

She lifts the duvet, and it acts as a shield between us. Ashley peers over the top of it, unsure of the next move. I can see complete confusion on her face. I wonder what goes through someone's mind when you wake up and there is a monkey in the bedroom. What could sensibly explain this particular scenario?

I have been here before, and now I have to make quick and correct decisions to avoid mistakes from the past. I look toward the bookshelf and see something that might help. With a leap, I grab a picture frame. Ashley screams at my sudden jump, but doesn't make any movement hinting at an escape. With the picture in my grasp, I rest on the floor in a crouched lotus position. I need to appear relaxed to calm Ashley. Surely, she will quickly realize a normal monkey wouldn't adopt the position of someone in prayer while holding a picture?

She stares at me with wide-open emerald eyes, her face utterly perplexed. The picture was taken at my brother Sidath's wedding. It depicts a smiling couple deeply in love. Ashley is wearing a light green lehenga adorned with gold patterned embroidery. She looks like a princess from an Arabian fairy tale, and perhaps that makes the tanned gentleman beside her a heroic Persian prince.

I point at the princess and then toward Ashley. Her mouth relaxes, not conveying an understanding of the situation but the realization that she senses something magical is afoot.

I then point at the picture image of my tanned former self and touch my face. I pause and then point at my monkey self. Ashley's face does not give any emotional response. She is frozen and has not made any movement.

She needs another piece of evidence, and I see it on her bedside table. I put the picture beside me, sit up, and hop onto the bed. She doesn't yelp in fear and seems more relaxed in my company. Perhaps she is giving me a moment to make my case, or perhaps she is readying herself to flee?

On the bedside table is a music player and a set of speakers. I recognize this device as I was the one who bought it for her. I also uploaded all the music onto it, so I am sure one song in particular will be present. I search for *Chicago* through the list of songs. She wanted this to be the soundtrack to our first dance at our wedding. It is one of the corniest songs you could ever imagine, so I was always a bit nervous about dancing in front of everyone we knew with *Glory of Love* playing in the background. I press play, and the song begins.

If there is one thing I am sure of, it is that Ashley knows a random monkey could not know our song. Whatever she believes, she knows this. How could an escaped stray monkey know that fact?

I stare at her, and finally, she makes a movement. After waking up to a monkey in her room, her perspective of reality finally becomes more lucid. She sits on the bed, and the song continues to play.

She drops the quilt, and I see she is wearing pink pajamas with a monkey face pattern. Ashley is a lover of monkeys, too. She's wearing the pajamas that I bought for her.

She opens her mouth and whispers, "Is it really you?"

36
MY EUREKA MOMENTS USUALLY COME ON THE TOILET

I nod, unable to speak in this realm. Hopefully, she will realize that yes and no are the limits of my communication.

"But how is this possible?" she asks.

Before I have a chance to offer an answer in sign language to this extremely difficult question, she raises her doubts.

"What am I thinking? Am I completely losing it? Perhaps I am still asleep. I will pinch myself and see if I wake up." She grabs hard at the flesh on her forearm and then cries with pain. Opening her eyes, she peers in my direction. For the first time in a long time, I feel naked, as if her glare is stripping me, but of course, I am naked except for a few tufts of fur.

"Okay, so this is not a dream. There really is a monkey in my room. That monkey seems rather calm and clever and likes to look at pictures of me and my ex-boyfriend. That same monkey also knows how to use a music player and picked the favorite song of my ex-boyfriend and mine. What does that prove?"

Why does she keep saying ex-boyfriend? I suppose my behavior before my attempted suicide would explain the end of our relationship.

Ashely continues, "Okay, so let's put this into perspective. I have a crazy hunch. You are a clever monkey but not clever enough to speak. I will ask you a series of questions, and you must answer them correctly. You can nod or shake your head or perform some sort of charade. If you get these correct, I will decide whether or not I'm having a nervous breakdown."

As our eyes meet, I smile the goofy, toothy smile of a primate. She always made me laugh when she was out of her comfort zone. Ashley is a control freak—an incessant planner—so I didn't get to see her thinking on her feet very often. She always comes across as calm and emotionally reserved, so inducing a breakdown is definitely not my intention.

She sits, considering her first question, but is almost silent apart from the noise of her breathing. Her eyes are shut, and she appears to be focused on the decision of how to begin. "Okay, question one. Where do you do most of your thinking?"

I know this answer. I do most of my thinking in the same place as every other man. I generally have my eureka moments on the toilet. I like to switch off the lights in the bathroom and sit in the darkness on the lavatory. Blackness and solitude are the perfect environment in which to relax and think.

Unable to answer this question with a simple movement of my head, I sit crouched as if on a potty and adopt a stern look. My eyebrows are like storm clouds on the horizon, and then I leap from the imaginary toilet seat and jump into the air as if I've just come up with a perfect solution to a problem, clutching at the victory in my hand. I prance around the room, forgetting where I am, lost in the performance as if the actual remedy to my reincarnation riddle is within my grasp. Being around Ashley has brought me so close to everything I have been hoping and dreaming of. *If I get the chance, I will make sure I put my heart into every moment we share together.*

Ashely coughs to get my attention, "Well, I gather from your performance that you were acting out sitting on the toilet, which is correct. However, lots of men—and it seems monkeys—think on the loo, so you have not proved anything yet." She lies face down on the bed, seemingly becoming more relaxed, and places her chin on the palm of her upturned hand.

"Question two. Did you love her?"

As she says this, no tears well up in her eyes and there is no obvious sadness etched on her face. The only change in her posture is that the palm on which her chin is resting becomes a fist. I shake my head and edge closer to her, but she rears up and moves to the back of the bed. The mattress width between us seems as impossible to traverse as the Atlantic Ocean separating the UK from Brazil.

She sternly addresses me, "A shake of the head suffices only because you cannot speak. Question three. Why did you try to kill yourself?"

Knowing a simple shake of the head will not suffice, I take a deep breath and consider what my next Marcel Marceau monkey mime performance will entail.

I point at Ashley and jump onto the bed. She leans back but does not retreat. I point to her stomach and then make a cradle in my arms.

"The baby!" Ashley's control over her emotions vanishes, and it is difficult to witness. However, these are the repercussions of my actions, and dealing with them is my only means of making up for my failures. I need to put right the wrongs of my past. I sit on the bed and wait for her sobbing to abate. I reach for her hand with mine, and on seeing this through sodden eyelashes, she cautiously accepts my grasp. I rub the top of her hand with my wrist and close my eyes. *I have traveled across time, through the maze of reality, and tested the realms of sanity to be with you, my love.*

Ashley weeps as she offers what I expect to be a sad summary of our desperate situation, "So, what now? I suppose we have resolved you are in fact now a monkey. Where do we go from here? You have been in a coma for the last twelve months. Everyone—including your family and the doctors—have given up on you ever recovering. The only reason we had any hope whatsoever was that you had periodic brain activity. I suppose the noises make sense now. You kept making monkey noises in your sleep... Little *ooh oohs* and *aah aahs*! But occasionally, you would scream loudly enough to wake the entire ward. For some reason, we all saw it as a sign of hope that something was still ticking away in that brain of yours, that you weren't completely drained of life.

"But in the last three months, there have been no signs of brain activity whatsoever. The doctors had to use electric shocks to keep you alive on two occasions. It was becoming too much for your mother to wait and hope. It was becoming too much for all of us... My life felt like it was wilting away, hopelessly waiting for you to return. Now you are too late. You waited too long."

I'm stunned. I was still alive up until yesterday.

Ashley can see that her words have shocked me and continues to explain, "Yesterday, they switched off your life support. You are dead. *Anil is dead.*"

37
FRAUDULENT CORPSES

How many times can one boy—excuse me, monkey boy—die? I have grown accustomed to the knowledge that I am no longer of this earth. Surely, the experiences of my last six months can only be explained as those of a being who is neither dead nor alive. However, meeting my father gave me hope that there might be a way back to my previous life. It seems as if the reincarnation process is complete, and my spirit has passed from Anil to Branko. If Ashley is correct, Anil is no more, and I am destined to remain in this primate's body until the last semblance of my human memory evaporates.

Ashley can see her news has deflated my enthusiasm. Knowing my sadness, I am sure she will offer some sort of consolation. "Do you want to see the body?"

This is not the uplifting opportunity I was hoping for from my ex-girlfriend. What will seeing my former vessel achieve? Do I really want to be confronted with my own corpse? Some of the worst memories of my life have been walking into funeral parlors to show my respects to the waxy-skinned shell of a loved one.

My first experience was when one of my school friends died at fifteen years old. His name was Vernon, and he went to the same school as me and lived around the corner. Rumors had passed around school that he had contracted meningitis. Rumor became fact, and in the space of three days, Vernon had become seriously ill and died.

When I heard news of his death, I walked around to his house. I refused to accept this morbid fact as truth. My naïve, youthful sense of right and wrong would not accept such a pernicious reality.

As I entered Vernon's family home, I saw a house filled with embarrassed people staring at the floor, ashamed to make eye contact. Vernon's mother saw me and ran to me, grabbing my young frame and clutching it as though I was the son she had lost. People used to tell me I looked like Vernon. That was an extremely generous compliment, as he was much more handsome than me.

I remember walking into the private room of the funeral parlor with my father beside me. I was not keen to attend, and my family didn't put any pressure on me, but I knew the right thing to do was say goodbye. Neither of us knew what to expect, but the person in the coffin was an imposter. A lifeless, stuffed puppet lying in an uncomfortable-looking box, pretending to be one of my childhood friends. I don't think my father had seen a child's cadaver before, and his silence betrayed his calm demeanor. Neither of us knew what to say, and so we said nothing at all.

Is it strange that the next time I saw a dead body, it was the person who accompanied me to see my first? When I walked into the funeral parlor and saw my father's inanimate body, I prayed for him to come back to life, just for a second, so I could tell him how much I loved him. I stood at the top of the coffin and hoped for a means of contacting him in the afterlife. I kissed his forehead and immediately noticed how hard and unlike flesh it felt. My dad's forehead felt like plastic. The dead bear no resemblance to the people who lived and were loved. I do not envy anyone who must go to see the deceased shell of a loved one. Even though it was an awful reality to confront, I must complete the circle and visit the resting place of my former body. It is the right thing to do.

I remember my bearings and focus on the beautiful brunette in front of me. She repeats her question, "Do you want to see your body?" I nod, knowing this is the final leg of my journey. I am making my funeral march a day late. I am being reunited with my corpse in an attempt to lay my soul to rest.

38
UGLY BABY

As we travel in the car, my mind is frantic about what approaches. Confronting my own deceased body seems to be the right next step, and yet I am quite sure it will mean the end of me. I am less aware of being in the car or watching the flitter of sunlight breaking through leafy skies. In fact, I feel unlike any time in our existence as Branko. Something inside me is ebbing away, about to be extinguished like a snuffed-out candle. As I stare at Ashley beside me, a desolate tear escapes my eye. I cannot rid my mind of the thought that this destiny is my creation. My mistakes brought me here, and this conclusion is due to my actions alone.

Then sleep overcomes me, and when I awake, what seems to be moments later, I am being carried in a warm blanket in a pretty girl's arms. She has a kind face and short brown hair. She looks down at me, and her green eyes glimmer with worry. I see our reflection in a shop window and encounter the strangest sight. I think I just saw the same woman running down the street with the ugliest baby you ever saw! It looked far too hairy to be human! I immediately felt sorry for the mother, who must have been horribly ashamed of the child.

The strange girl carrying me reaches a doorway and bursts through. We are overcome by the smell of scented candles and joss sticks. Someone is trying to hide the scent of death in this place.

A large lady stands up and pleasantly greets the pretty girl, "Hello, my dear, I wasn't expecting you until the cremation tomorrow. Ah, have you brought a baby along? May I have a look? He is soo—AAAARRRRRGGGGGHHHH!" The large lady seems to have taken a sudden nap on the floor.

The pretty girl sidesteps the large, sleeping woman and makes her way into a side room. It is a gaping hollow space that opens from an impossibly small door. The décor in this room is quite repulsive. There are plastic, white flowers littered around, and the air is thick with the scent of the burning candles and incense. The room is dimly lit, and the color of the carpet is purple and resembles blackcurrant vomit if a blackcurrant was capable of being sick. The room is empty apart from several tables with flower vases adorning them, circling an unusual rectangular box standing on a waist-high platform in the middle of the room.

The pretty girl is crying now, perhaps due to the color of the carpet, and approaches the large wooden box. A tear from the girl falls on my head, and I contemplate what I did to deserve being rained upon by this angel. We reach the box, which appears to be open, and I am too tired for the horror to overcome me. The pretty girl whispers into my ear, "It is you, baby." Her words confuse and anger me and yet I know she is right. I must return to my destiny.

My brother told me to accept the past as it was my only means back to reality. My father instructed me to make the right choices to rectify the damage caused by my past poor decisions. Now, my final decision is to relieve Branko of his burden and to return to my present incapacitated state. I must accept a return to my corpse to end the chaos I have caused in this world and the afterlife.

I tug at the angel's arm from within her cuddling embrace, and she leans toward me. I look into her emerald-green eyes, hoping she can see my soul within this unfamiliar shell. I raise my head and kiss her cheek, seeing the trail of a teardrop and promising never to hurt her again.

She rests me on the chest of my former self's cadaver, and I relinquish myself from the clutch of the blanket. A momentary last glimpse of the reality I have created. I stare at the lifeless piece of meat before me. *Why did you do it? Why did you throw it all away? You had a great life, but you destroyed it and everything around you.*

There is nothing left but to leave the weeping cherub with another tragedy on her hands. My father thought there was a chance for my survival, but I was too late. His last advice was to choose the right path. I know my final act will lead to tragedy. At this last moment, for the first time in my life, I am not my first priority. I am dead and am finally free of the selfish attitude that shadowed me throughout my existence. My last choice will be to bid farewell to life. I have been given a chance to say goodbye to Ashley and release her and everyone from my burden. How I long to bid farewell to my family, but they have already gone through enough since my attempted and eventually achieved suicide.

I edge to the forehead of my former body and perform the last act of the boy in the monkey. The Anil Perera I knew died a long time ago, and now we shall rest in peace together. I kiss his—my—forehead and am gone.

39
MONKEY FOUND IN FUNERAL PARLOUR

NEWS REPORT – DAILY LONDON TIMES. 15 MAY 2001.

Yesterday, a British man, who had been declared dead after being in a coma for nearly a year, has woken up in a funeral parlour in London.

The un-named man, 20, was declared dead after twelve months of lying in a coma after a fall from a bridge. He had been in a vegetative state for the last three months, and the decision was made to remove him from life support a few days ago. He was then transported to the funeral parlour, where he had apparently lain deceased.

To make matters even more interesting, on the evening of the re-awakening, one of the proprietors of the funeral parlour phoned the police to report a break-in.

When police arrived on the scene, they found an ecstatic girl, the former corpse alive and awake, and the owner of the funeral parlour catatonically unconscious. Additionally, police reported the formerly dead man was holding the body of a monkey when they found him. Yes, you read that right, *holding the body of a monkey.*

The recovered man had no comment and is currently undergoing medical examination. He has claimed to be suffering from amnesia, and doctors state that this is a possible side effect of his coma. The police have no rational explanation for the events but are continuing their investigation and will be questioning the man when he is released from medical care.

We have been unable to gain any response from the proprietor of the funeral parlour and cannot begin to explain the circumstances surrounding this 'miracle.' A somewhat unusual repercussion to events, the funeral parlour has become a magnet for religious fanatics. People who follow faiths ranging from Christianity, Hinduism, and Voodoo have all paid their respects to the source of this modern-day second coming.

Whipps Cross Hospital, based in East London, has confirmed the man was pronounced dead on the 14th of May, 2001.

London Zoo has stated that none of their primates have recently escaped from their enclosures.

40
TRAGEDY LEADS TO NEW BEGINNINGS

I am standing in front of the monkey enclosure at the London Zoo. Ashley is with me. She detests zoos and has only attended because I have begged her to come. Since Branko's funeral, everyone has been treating me with trepidation. It seems as if no one knows what I will do next.

I felt tremendously depressed in the first week after his funeral. I would wake up in the middle of the night and feel like something was moving around my bedroom. I would feel a flick behind my ear that would wake me from slumber. It was somewhat similar to when my dad passed on. I never felt as if I was truly alone. However, I dared not to let anyone in on the secret that my father was still with me in case it meant he might leave.

An odd thing happened in the house as I mourned my little monkey brother. When I tried to stroke either of my pet family cats, they would hiss at me and run out of the house. My mum was disappointed; she loves those cats almost as much as her sons.

Another very odd occurrence occurred when I visited my brother's house last week. It was the first time I had ventured to see my niece Ava since I had awoken. It has been over a year since I laid eyes on her, and she is quickly becoming a mischievous toddler. Amal picked up her favorite toy, the monkey I gave her for her first birthday. He called to Ava and said, "Where's monkey?" Her ears and eyes perked up as she stood in the middle of the living room, but rather than run over to Amal, she ran over to me and hugged my leg. When I sat on the floor beside her, she gave me a big, sloppy kiss and then sat back and smiled a toothy grin. A toddler of two years old had answers to the questions lurking in the shadows. It was so obvious, and yet I was in a state of confusion due to the mourning process.

Ava hasn't said many sentences yet, but as she looked at me, she said, "You are a silly monkey."

At the zoo today, the sun is hidden by clouds typical of a British summer, but the air is refreshing. The wind carries a slight chill, so I take a swig from a hip flask sitting in the inner pocket of my tweed jacket. I look at Ashley and take another hit.

"Anil, is everything okay? Should you really be drinking at this time of the day? It is only just after ten in the morning."

"Honestly, bubba, this is actually quite late for me! Normally I have had a double-double by nine. Anyway, it is not alcohol, it is a banana milkshake." I have decided to abstain from alcohol for the moment. I am determined to get to the bottom of my feelings, and alcohol only serves to cloud my judgment.

I consider my next step very carefully. I need her to know my true feelings, and sometimes actions speak louder than words.

I shout to the universe and my dearest love, "Look, baby, I brought you here for a special reason. Since I went away, I have changed. Being in the jungle and out of my body gave me a new perspective on life. I know we said goodbye to Branko last week but—" I don't know how to put my feelings into words. I start doing a little jig in front of the enclosure. I prance along the ground, bounce up and down, scratch my head, and make some characteristic monkey noises. It seems I haven't lost all of my primate traits. The monkeys in the enclosure understand my comments and ready themselves for the action ahead.

Ashley gives me a similar look to the one she gave Branko when she first met him in her bedroom, "Anil, are you okay? You are acting quite strangely. Do I need to call your doctor? Stop monkeying around!"

I chuckle and respond, "Bubba Turk, this is why I love you. I am acting strangely, and you have the strength to tell me that. The truth is I have always been strange, and life will just get stranger. Can you deal with me? Can you deal with that? The fact is that I am not just Anil anymore, but I am Branko as well— we are one. You will be spending your life with a part boy, part monkey. A monkeyboy, a freak of nature, a priman, a chimpboyzee, a mankey, a boychimp!"

Ashley looks at me, smiles, and says, "I have no words."

I shout again to the powers that be, letting them know that, for the first time in my life, I understand how I fit and where I'm headed. "Don't say anything; just listen. I love you. Branko loves you. We want you to marry us. We want a family. We already know our children's names. They will be named Lillian and Rosanna. We will have a cat called Erika and a dog called Kandy, but that's way down the line. Let's not get ahead of ourselves. We can go to Brazil for our honeymoon. I know a lovely couple there who will take great care of us. I also know a elephant who will be extremely glad to see us. Just hold your answer for one moment—"

Before she can answer, I pull out a pair of garden secateurs and cut through the wires of the monkey's enclosure. First in monkey jibber and then in human talk, I say, "No monkey shall be incarcerated in these prisons without trial! I stand for integrity. I will always do the right thing and my family shall have dignity! I will free them in your honor, my brother Branko!"

The frenzied excitement of my comrades' release fills my ears, I take Ashley's hands, and we run from the zoo guards, laughing like children.

Branko will always be in my heart, as from now to forever the monkey shall be in the boy.

THE END

ABOUT THE AUTHOR

Anil Kurukulasooriya was born in London to Sri Lankan parents and is rumored to be of royal lineage. He has lived in London for the majority of his life apart from attending University in Manchester and Bristol. He studied Geography and then Law before qualifying as a solicitor. He began writing his debut novel when living in Vienna after a youth obsessing about primates. When he's not writing, he is a dedicated father and husband who also enjoys boxing, long-distance running, and poetry.

Anil's next book, *Sledgehammer*, will be released in 2025.

Tag along on his adventures!
- *Instagram:* @kuruvision
- *X:* @kingkongkuru

Printed in Great Britain
by Amazon

60879007R00087